I'd Like to Thank my
Husband for joining me
on this Crazy Adventure

Books By
Joanne Keele

Dreams Collection
- Dreams
- Dreaming
- Living

Living

Chapter One
A Race to find Katrina

The situation surrounding McMatters, Jarvis, and Lorraine is fraught with a palpable urgency with the escalating tension as they unite in a frantic effort to locate Katrina. The car that recently held her captive in its boot had seemingly vanished into thin air, leaving behind an unsettling mystery. This vehicle an old silver, aging BMW that displays the marks of neglect with its fading colour and rusted areas, which only serves to deepen the sense of foreboding that envelops the search party. It is abundantly clear to them that this ominous car was lurking somewhere nearby, waiting for nightfall to execute its sinister plot and transport Katrina to an undisclosed location, which is shrouded in secrecy and fear. This grim reality raises several critical questions that gnaw at their minds: where exactly was this elusive car hiding? Who had taken Katrina in the first place? What were their malevolent intentions for her once they reached their unknown destination? In a desperate bid to find answers and reclaim hope, the family of the missing woman has mobilised their own search teams. Blythe's sister, who shares familial ties, but also an emotional bond with Jarvis, he has taken on a leading role in this harrowing endeavour. Some of the crews are scouring the streets on foot, stopping every passer-by with fervent determination in hopes of grasping any fragment of information, that might lead them closer to her whereabouts.

Their inquiries are tinged with desperation as they seek even the slightest clue or hint about Katrina's fate. Meanwhile, others are driving through the neighbourhoods with eyes peeled for any sign of the mysterious vehicle or its occupants; each glance at parked cars had become laden with anticipation and dread, Jarvis was trying hard to keep his head screwed on, and emotions in check. Concurrently, certain groups expanded their search radius further afield, perhaps hoping that by casting a wider net, they might uncover vital leads or evidence left unnoticed in less frequented areas.

As twilight casts long shadows across the landscape, darkness encroaching swiftly upon them like a predator stalking its prey, time transforms into an increasingly daunting adversary. The mounting pressure amplifies the sense of desperation felt by all involved; every tick of the clock serves as a stark reminder that they are racing against time itself... a relentless force threatening to seal Katrina's fate within an ever-narrowing window of opportunity for rescue. The weight of uncertainty hangs heavily over them, as hope battles despair amidst surreal circumstances fraught with danger at every turn.

Team Gastro and Hailstorm were on foot, tirelessly assisting with the urgent search for Katrina, who had been missing for far too long. Their hearts raced with a mix of anxiety and determination as they navigated the bustling streets, desperately seeking any leads that might illuminate her whereabouts. They approached a woman on the corner of a busy intersection, their eyes filled with hope as they asked if she might know anything about Katrina's disappearance. With every moment that passed, the stakes grew higher; time was not on their side. They needed to uncover any clues... something she might have seen... heard... anything that could guide them closer to finding her before it was too late.

"Hello, I'm sorry for disturbing you but our friend has been kidnapped. We are searching to try and find something that could help us to locate her. Have you seen a silver BMW, a rust bucket... heard screams... anything?"

"Umm, well, one block over, I saw a silver car pull into a garage with one of those roll-up doors. The only reason it stood out is that after I crossed over to this block, I heard a shout that sounded odd. I don't know if it helps?"

"Thank you! Thank you! It's a big help."

Darkness had fallen, enveloping everything in a heavy shroud that thickened the air around them. They understood with urgency that time was of the essence. Every passing moment increased the risk of critical information slipping through their fingers. They needed to get the word out swiftly and efficiently to close in on the location before it vanished from their grasp. With every heartbeat, apprehension pulsed through them; all that stood between them and success was a network of communication that must be activated without delay. The stakes were high, and failure was not an option… her life hung in the balance as they scrambled to relay crucial details to those who could help. Gastro and Hailstorm dashed to the block with urgency, their hearts racing as they reached the corner. They quickly positioned themselves strategically, maintaining a vigilant lookout for any unusual activity that could indicate trouble. As they stood there, tension crackled in the air around them, each moment amplifying their need to act swiftly. With a firm grip on their phones, they made the critical calls, ensuring all the details were conveyed clearly, while remaining hyper-aware of their surroundings. The stakes were high; they knew that what happened next could change everything.

"Jarvis, did you get the message out about my location. I'm standing on the corner, watching the block where a woman heard loud noises and saw a silver car. I'm opposite the town hall gardens," said Hailstorm.

"Great work. I'm on my way," said Jarvis.

While Hailstorm was anxiously on the phone with Jarvis, a sense of urgency filled the air as Gastro frantically flagged down anyone within reach, desperate to gather any crucial intel that might help their situation. He managed to catch the attention of Charlie and Delta, waving his arms in an exaggerated manner, signalling for them to come over quickly. They spotted the leader of the Bennetts driving past and began waving frantically, their hearts racing as they hoped to attract his attention before it was too late. The streets were bustling with activity; most people either driving or walking belonged to one of the families involved, making every moment feel like a race against time. Each passing car heightened Gastro's anxiety, amplifying his worry that valuable information could slip away just when they needed it most. The atmosphere was charged with tension as they desperately sought answers amidst an environment filled with familiar faces but potentially hidden dangers.

Chapter Two
Gathering

Jarvis arrived on the scene to find all the families and crew members huddled together in a large, anxious cluster. The sight was both chaotic and concerning, with palpable tension in the air. Jarvis understood that this gathering could easily draw law enforcement's attention, complicating an already precarious situation. Realising the potential repercussions of their conspicuous assembly, he knew he had to act swiftly and strategically to disperse the crowd. With urgency coursing through his veins, he shouted for them to blend into their surroundings. It was crucial to minimize visibility, to avoid any unwelcome scrutiny from passing police officers who might mistake their gathering for something more sinister. The stakes were high, and Jarvis was acutely aware that every moment counted in maintaining their safety and discretion.

"OK, can we split up? I want this block covered in every direction. No more than five in a group. I want all the leaders with me."

Everyone scattered quickly, each instinctively seeking a section to cover, driven by an urgent sense of necessity. The air was thick with tension, and anxiety hung over them like a dark cloud. In their haste, they broke off in different directions, fully aware that every second counted. The urgency reminded them that in a crisis, decision-making often feels rushed and frantic. Careful consideration of their surroundings became paramount as they navigated the chaos; one wrong move could lead to further complications or unforeseen dangers. Each knew it was vital to remain vigilant and focused amidst the whirlwind, a crucial reminder that in moments of urgency, clarity can easily be obscured by panic. As the leaders approached one of the two rolling shutters on the block, a sense of foreboding settled over them. At first glance, the building seemed entirely unoccupied, and disused for many years, it was shrouded in an oppressive darkness that swallowed any hint of life or activity within. The air was thick with an unsettling stillness, highlighted by crumbling outer walls that bore witness to years of neglect and decay. The rusted shutter hung limply, a grim barrier hinting at a time when this place might have thrived as a bustling car parts shop. Now, it stood as a haunting reminder of abandonment and desolation, a stark warning about what happens when neglect takes hold. They were on their way to examine another building with a shuttered facade. This structure, while rundown, was not in as dire a state as the previous building they had just inspected. The earlier site, once a thriving glass shop according to the overhead sign, now stood abandoned and forlorn, its windows shattered and entrance choked with weeds. As they approached the next building, a sense of caution washed over them; the peeling paint and sagging roof hinted at years of neglect, it certainly didn't look like it was a safe building.

As they approached the front of the second building, an unsettling noise reached their ears, high pitched noise that hurt the ears, a sound reminiscent of something stiffly creaking and moving in the shadows. Jarvis, sensing that something was amiss, instinctively turned to investigate the source of the disturbance. To his surprise and alarm, he noticed that the shutter on the first building had suddenly sprung to life, revealing a swift movement just beyond its confines. In a matter of moments, an old silver BMW burst forth from its hiding place, speeding away with an urgency that raised countless questions. The situation felt oddly foreboding; what or who had been inside that building? Why did it leave in such haste? The air was thick with tension as they stood there, grappling with a sense of unease about what this unexpected event could mean for their safety and plans moving forward.

"After that car! Go, Go, Go!" shouted McMatters.

Men all over the parking lot sprinted towards their cars with a fervent urgency, driven by a desperate hope to catch up with the old BMW, it was still moving at an alarming speed considering its age. Their hurried movements were not entirely devoid of caution; there was an underlying tension in the air, as if they were racing against time itself. The old car represented not just a mode of transport, but a symbol of status and the successful kidnapping of Katrina, igniting an instinctual urge to pursue it at any cost. The clamour of slamming doors and revving engines filled the air, creating a chaotic symphony that underscored the urgency of their mission.

Chapter Three
The Race

Every crew member sprang into action, racing toward their cars with urgency and determination. Their hearts pounded not just from adrenaline, but also from the weight of their mission: to join their families in pursuing the elusive old silver BMW, that had suddenly drawn their attention. Despite its age, its once shiny exterior now dulled and marked by time, the vehicle was darting through traffic weaving in and out at with impressive speeds, that belied its years. As they merged onto the expressway, a convoy of vehicles formed, each driven by an anxious crew member, each equally invested in this high-stakes chase. The roar of engines filled the air, harmonising with the frantic beeping of horns, as they navigated through lanes, weaving in and out like a school of fish evading danger. The thrill was both exciting and frightening. It was not just a simple drive... it was a collective effort fuelled by urgency and shared purpose, as they all sought answers to why this car's occupants had taken Katrina in the first place, surly they would have known the consequences of kidnapping someone who was family to the mafia, was not only stupid and reckless one of the worst moves to make, they always find you it's just a matter of time.

They understood the gravity of the situation; Katrina's life hung precariously in the balance, teetering on the edge of uncertainty. As the sleek silver BMW merged onto the motorway, a sense of urgency filled the air. Following closely behind was a convoy of cars, each brimming with anxiety and determination. The drivers exchanged anxious glances, their hearts racing with hope and fear alike. They all shared a singular purpose: to find a way to stop that car before it was too late, clinging to the slim possibility that Katrina was still alive and could be saved from whatever peril she faced inside that vehicle. The stakes were high, and every second counted as they navigated through traffic in pursuit of her safety.

As Jarvis settled into his seat and gazed out of the window, he began to wonder where they were driving, a question that nagged at the back of his mind like an elusive puzzle piece. McMatters, leading the convoy, navigated down the motorway, leaving Jarvis both curious and somewhat anxious about their destination. This unexpected journey offered him a unique opportunity to engage with the other families around him. He struck up conversations, listening intently as they shared their thoughts and feelings about the trip ahead. Each family member's voice added another layer to the tapestry of uncertainty surrounding them...a blend of excitement, apprehension, and hope hanging in the air like an unspoken agreement.

As they drove further into unknown territory, Jarvis tried to piece together clues from their conversations, gathering snippets of information that might hint at their eventual location. With each exchange, he juggled possibilities in his mind: Were they headed toward a long-awaited reunion? A much-needed retreat? Or perhaps something entirely unexpected? The road stretched on before them like an open book waiting to be written upon, each mile bringing new questions, and potential answers swirling around in his thoughts. Jarvis opened a Team call.

"Santos, Bennetts, Blythe, and my guys you are all on a call as we need to work out where we are heading, all ideas are welcome," said Jarvis.

"Well, what have we got in this direction? I mean we have the peak district depending on if they change motorways a little further up," said Santos.

"We have an airport on this stretch," said Blythe.

"What about the docks?" asked Bennett.

"Let's keep thinking and reach out to any contacts in those areas. They might know of places that might be of interest," said Jarvis.

Jarvis placed the phone down. Lorraine and McMatters turned their attention to solving the puzzle, their expressions reflecting a mix of curiosity and contemplation. The three of them were silent, lost in thought as they pondered the merits and potential drawbacks of each location they were considering. They weighed factors such as accessibility, atmosphere, and available amenities, envisioning how each place could serve their specific needs. This collaborative moment, filled with earnest discussion, underscored the importance of making an informed decision together as a team.

"I can't see them heading into the country. It's too easy for us to follow them. They will want to vanish quickly, so I'd say somewhere more built-up, but not as busy as the airport, unless they have their own plane, which I doubt very much," said Jarvis.
"So, you're thinking the docks?"
"Maybe. I see Bennett's guy is at the docks in this direction."
Jarvis gets on the phone to Bennett.
"Bennett, can you reach out to your guy at the docks on the stretch we're on? Ask him to watch for an old silver BMW. That way, if we lose them, we will know if they go there."
"Yes, will do. Is that what you're thinking?"
"Yes. I don't know why, but I have a hunch."

Chapter Four
They got away

When they finally peeled off the motorway, the silver BMW decided it was time to channel its inner race car driver, putting the pedal to the metal in a valiant attempt to zoom through the now red traffic lights. "Shit!" shouted McMatters, his annoyance bubbling over like a pot of water left unattended on the stove. He was not just mildly irritated; he was practically seething, the lights had conspired against him, turning from amber to crimson in what felt like an instant, leaving him trapped. It was as if the traffic signals had declared a personal vendetta against his impeccable timing! Around fourteen cars, like a rogue parade of mismatched clowns, were tailing them in a chaotic procession. Each vehicle was part of the crew. An eclectic mix of makes and models, on a madcap race to save Katrina. Cars with engines roaring like they were auditioning for a rock concert, it was an absurd scene straight out of an action movie where even the GPS seemed confused, trying to navigate this motley crew through what felt like an obstacle course, designed by someone who had just binge-watched too many car chase films!

And now, the fate of Katrina is once again in the hands of the animals who have her, they've completely lost track of the silver BMW. It's like trying to find a needle in a haystack. Jarvis, clearly channelling his inner action hero, jumped onto the phone conference call with all the urgency of someone who just spilled coffee on their favourite shirt.

"Listen up!" he exclaimed dramatically. "I need everyone to ring everyone they know in this area… your Aunt Patty, your best friend from college, even that guy who always seems to know where the best tacos are! I need intel and I need it yesterday! Start the search; we've lost them!"

Thirty minutes later, Bennett calls on the Team call with a sense of urgency that could wake a sloth from its nap.

"Get to the dockyard!" he barks into the phone before hanging up, as if he just dropped a bombshell. Suddenly, it's like someone set off a starter pistol at a race; all you see is a chaotic swarm of cars erupting into motion, spinning and swerving toward the dockyard faster than you could say "traffic jam." It's as if every driver suddenly decided that obeying speed limits was an optional suggestion rather than a rule. Horns blaring and tires screeching, it's clear that this isn't just any ordinary drive, it was a race to find the kidnappers and save Katrina before they made her vanish forever.

Chapter Five
The Dockyard

They arrive at the dockyard, and with a sense of urgency, Jarvis command, "Gastro and Hailstorm, you two need to block their exit immediately… no one gets past you! Everyone else… spread out; we have a vast area to cover here. Bennett, I want you to check in with your contact. Find out if he spotted which direction they headed. We can't let them slip away."
"On it."

And so, the arduous and seemingly impossible search for Katrina begins. A true needle-in-a-haystack endeavour, fraught with challenges and uncertainty. Each passing moment weighs heavily on the hearts of those involved, as they cling to a fragile thread of hope that she will be located safe, alive, and in one piece. The determination to uncover her whereabouts drives the searchers forward, fuelled by a fierce resolve that refuses to wane. Every clue, no matter how small or seemingly insignificant, becomes a beacon of possibility in this daunting quest for answers.

"Jarvis. They were seen on the right-side before they were lost between the containers."
"Thanks Bennett."

Row by row, aisle by aisle, the seemingly endless expanse of identical containers loomed before Jarvis, an overwhelming sight that filled him with a sense of dread. Each container appeared just like the last, their uniformity creating an impenetrable maze, that felt both disorienting and claustrophobic. As he navigated this daunting landscape of steel and shadows, a chilling thought consumed his mind: what if they had placed her inside one of these countless containers? How could anyone possibly locate her in such a vast sea of anonymity? The reality was stark and terrifying;

every second spent searching was a second too late. The urgency to uncover her whereabouts grew ever more pressing as Jarvis grappled with the fear that time might slip away from him like sand through his fingers.

From the corner of her eye, Lorraine caught a flicker of movement that danced tantalisingly at the edge of her vision. Though she couldn't quite decipher what it was, one thing was certain: they had to investigate further.

"Turn right quick," she barked with urgency, her voice cutting through the tension in the air. "Straight right again here! I saw something move!"

The determination in her tone underscored the seriousness of the situation, compelling everyone to act swiftly and decisively, as curiosity mingled with caution in their hearts. Another car in the group noticed the abrupt change in direction and decisively followed suit. The driver, fully aware of the situation, quickly adjusted their steering to align with the new trajectory. This instinctive response, not only demonstrated a keen awareness, but also a readiness to adapt to unforeseen circumstances on the road. As a result, the movement of this vehicle became part of an orchestrated manoeuvre, reflecting a collective understanding among the drivers, that swift action was necessary in such dynamic scenarios.

"Spread out and search all of them if you have to," Jarvis commanded. His voice cutting through the air, as he gestured toward the towering freight containers, that loomed like sentinels at the edge of the yard. The urgency in his tone spurred more individuals from their initial positions; one by one, they began to converge on the scene, after spotting the containers from a distance. As they organised themselves, some members of the group circled around the massive structures, their footsteps echoing softly against the metal surfaces, while others boldly approached those on the ground level and began prying them open with determination. To maintain a clear record of their progress amidst this chaotic search effort, they made it a point to leave each opened container slightly ajar. A subtle, but effective method to signal which ones had already been inspected. Three men came back, dragging two men with them.

"We found these close by, but they have no ID on them. I don't think they belong here," said foxtrot.

They stayed quiet until McMatters stood next to them. He gestured for them to be stood upright, and hit one of them repeatedly. Jarvis could see that McMatters was having fun, so he started on the other one. McMatters and Jarvis stayed quiet. Not a single word was spoken. Once they got to a specific point, the guys with no ID were struggling to focus.

"So, lads, whoever speaks first and tells me where she is will get to live" said McMatters.
"547" one of them said before passing out.

Everyone frantically raced against the clock, to locate container five four seven. Their urgency palpable in the atmosphere. Amidst this chaotic search, the individual who had provided the crucial number was unceremoniously placed into a car, unconscious and oblivious to the frenzy unfolding around them. Meanwhile, another person, a key participant in this high-stakes situation was momentarily held up, anxiously waiting for further information that would lead them to container five four seven. The tension of the moment hung heavy, with time slipping away, as they grappled with both confusion and determination.

After what felt like an eternity of searching, they finally discovered the container and flung open its heavy doors. Inside, they were met with the sight of an old silver BMW, a beacon of hope amidst the chaos. Without wasting a moment,

Jarvis dashed to the boot and yanked it open with a crowbar, a sense of urgency could be seen with each of his movements. There was Katrina, unconscious Jarvis checked her pulse, alive; her pulse was faint yet reassuringly present beneath his fingertips. Jarvis took a moment to breathe, he noticed he had been holding his breath. With determination fuelling his every move, Jarvis scooped her up effortlessly in his arms and carried her out of the confined space, resolute in his mission to ensure her safety and bring her back from the brink.

"That little fucker… put him in the boot," said Jarvis.

His crew did exactly what Jarvis wanted them to do. They put one of Slaters crew in the boot, closed the lid, locked the container, and walked away. With a sense of urgency, Jarvis carefully placed Katrina into the car, ensuring she was secure and comfortable. Lorraine occupied the front passenger seat alongside McMatters, who was gripping the steering wheel with determination. Meanwhile, Jarvis nestled Katrina in his arms in the back seat, his protective instincts overriding everything else as they sped toward the hospital. The thrum of the engine echoed in his ears while he focused intently on Katrina's fading breaths. Each moment feeling like an eternity, Katrina was in bad shape, they raced against time to provide her with the medical attention she desperately needed.

Chapter Six
Katrina

They arrived at the hospital, and although Katrina's pulse was still weak and faint, Jarvis felt an overwhelming sense of gratitude as he realised, she, indeed, still had one. Amidst the chaos of the emergency room and the palpable tension in the air, he clung to the flicker of hope represented by her heartbeat. Each thump reminded him of her resilience and strength, a testament to her will to fight against adversity. As medical professionals rushed around them with urgency and a focused determination, Jarvis silently vowed to remain by her side every step of the way, Jarvis didn't know where the feelings came from because he had only met her once before. McMatters felt a wave of surprise and disappointment when he realised that Blythe was not at the hospital, especially given the seriousness of Katrina's condition. With her life hanging in the balance, it seemed unfathomable that Katrina's own brother would choose to be absent at such a critical moment. The memory of Blythe lingered in McMatters' mind, vividly recalling their time at the dockyard, and when they were searching the streets. Blythe had stood there, seemingly lost and gormless, his face an expressionless mask devoid of urgency or emotion, as he processed the dire situation unfolding around him. Blythe had been physically present at the dockyard, yet McMatters couldn't shake the feeling that his presence was more about maintaining appearances, than genuine concern for his sister's wellbeing. Even when crucial help was needed, like opening the container doors to potentially save Katrina, Blythe remained passive, almost paralysed by indecision or apathy. It was disheartening for McMatters to witness such a lack of action from someone who should have been fighting tooth and nail for family, McMatters thought back at Blythe's actions and appearances, he couldn't recall Blythe showing any emotion which was most defiantly odd. Leaving him questioning not only

Blythe's priorities, but also his capacity for love and loyalty in times of crisis, as well as his position as head of the family. Lorraine took on the responsibility of overseeing the club, knowing it was where she was needed most, while McMatters stayed by Katrina's side, ensuring she was well cared for during Jarvis's distress. McMatters needed to keep a close eye on Jarvis, to prevent any impulsive actions arising from his emotional turmoil. Meanwhile, Bennett proved to be an asset in this chaotic situation; his leadership skills shone as he adeptly directed everyone involved. With a calm demeanour and clear instructions, he ensured all attendees left safely and in good spirits.

Bennett ensured Lorraine's safe return home by coordinating with her bodyguards. His dedication highlighted the value of teamwork in tough times. Once the nurse confirmed her stability, with normal breathing and heart rate, it was evident the medical team was performing well. They kept the oxygen mask on until she fully awakened, demonstrating their commitment to care. McMatters displayed great attention when moving Katrina to a private room, ensuring her comfort and privacy during recovery.

Chapter Seven
Lorraine

Lorraine had the club running like a well-oiled machine, it was one of her many skills. They were open for business tonight, and everything was buzzing with energy. Generally, they liked to have at least one boss around, just in case any issues popped up. With Lorraine at the helm, everyone felt reassured and ready for a fun night ahead! McMatters phoned to see if he was needed.

"Lorraine, how's it going?"
"We're good. The club is rocking. How is Katrina?"
"She's out of danger. Everything looks good, and she should be waking up soon."
"And Jarvis?"
"He's concerned for Katrina. He'll be better once she wakes up."
"That's good, because there's something I wanted to mention."
"Oh?"
"Blythe has been acting odd today. He was distant while we were searching for her, and has been vacant ever since."
"Funny you should say that, because he hasn't been to the hospital at all."
"Why would he not want to see her? She's, his sister."
"My thoughts exactly. I think we all need to talk about Blythe once Katrina is awake. I'll get the leaders together for a meeting. Well, everyone except Blythe."
"Yep, I think it's needed."
"I'll come back soon. It's been one hell of a day."
"See you soon, Steve."
"And you Lorraine. Bye."

Lorraine lounged back in her comfy chair, sipping on something delightfully unexpected. A drink called the Nipple Twister. As she took a sip, her taste buds danced with the sweet and tropical flavours that burst forth. She could easily pick out the fruity notes of strawberry Malibu, blending harmoniously with the tangy raspberry sours. And if she wasn't mistaken, there was a subtle hint of passion fruit juice weaving its way through the mix, adding an exotic flair to each refreshing gulp. It was twisted in flavour, but oh boy, was it nice! The drink felt like a mini-vacation in a glass, making her forget about the day's stresses while she savoured every drop.

Her thoughts drifted back to Blythe. She couldn't help but wonder what on earth was going on with him. When Katrina had been taken, he had been right there, stepping in to help her bit by bit. But as the day wore on, it seemed like he was becoming less and less responsive, which was not a good sign for someone in his position as a leader. His men, however, thankfully managed to stay focused and followed the directives given by Jarvis and Bennett without hesitation. Lorraine knew that they would need to come up with a plan regarding Blythe's behaviour; it seemed everyone could feel that something needed to be done about him before things spiralled further out of control.

Chapter Eight
Jarvis

Jarvis felt a deep sense of worry and concern for Katrina, especially after the harrowing ordeal she had endured. Her face bore the marks of her suffering, with bruises just showing the outlines of bad bruises yet to come, the rest of her body showed the pain across her body; it was as if every bruise told a story of struggle and resilience. With her features swollen and tender, he sat patiently by her side, waiting for her to awaken from her troubled slumber. The nurse had gently explained that Katrina's experience was not only physically exhausting, but also mentally draining, leaving invisible scars on her psyche. The nurse reassured him that the more rest she could obtain during this critical time, the better her chances of making a full recovery. Jarvis understood that sleep was not just a comfort; it was crucial for healing both body and mind. As he watched over Katrina, he hoped each peaceful breath would bring her closer to healing and restoration. Jarvis felt an overwhelming sense of compassion for Katrina, that he couldn't quite explain. It was as if an invisible thread had woven them together from the moment they first met. Igniting a deep instinct within him, to protect her at all costs. The pull of this connection was both comforting and perplexing; even though they had only just crossed paths, Jarvis couldn't imagine ever leaving her side. Each time he glanced at her, he felt his heart swell with a desire to shield her from harm or sorrow, as though their souls were already intertwined by some profound force, that transcended mere acquaintance. This inexplicable bond filled him with warmth and urgency, compelling him to stay close and be there for her in whatever way she might need. Jarvis glanced wearily at the clock on the wall; its hands stubbornly fixed on four in the morning. The room was steeped in a heavy silence, broken only by the soft hum of the night. Despite the early hour, there were no signs of life from her; she remained ensconced in sleep, cocooned beneath layers of blankets, as if she was shielding herself from the world outside. Each passing minute felt like an eternity to Jarvis as he held his breath, hoping for any sign she might wake soon. His heart ached with concern and longing; he yearned for her eyes to flutter open and bring colour back into this muted scene. The night felt endless and heavy with uncertainty, but he remained steadfast by her side, filled with unwavering hope that dawn would bring her back to him. Katrina had been in the hospital for what felt like an eternity…eight long hours, that stretched into a lifetime of uncertainty and anxiety. Each minute dragged on, heavy with worries and fears about her health, and yet, amidst all this turmoil, there was an even greater disappointment gnawing at her unconscious heart: the absence of her brother. Blythe, who had always been a pillar of support, had not shown his face even once during this agonising wait, this was like a red rag to a bull with Jarvis, Blythe's absence was not un-noted. His absence felt like a cold shadow looming over Katrina in her time of need.

Chapter Nine
Hospital

Bennett arrived at the hospital, his heart racing with a mix of concern and determination as he made his way to check on Katrina. After spending some time at home to freshen up and recharge with a few precious hours of sleep, he felt slightly more prepared to face the situation that awaited him. The sterile scent of antiseptic filled the air as he reached Katrina's room, where the atmosphere was heavy with worry, yet simultaneously illuminated by hope. As he stepped inside, his eyes immediately fell upon Jarvis, who was still steadfastly stationed by Katrina's side. Time seemed to stand still for him, as if he hadn't budged an inch since she had been rushed in for treatment. Bennett could sense the deep bond they shared; it was evident that Jarvis's presence provided comfort during this challenging moment. In a quiet corner of the room, McMatters had chosen to stay alongside Jarvis, offering silent support and solidarity. The sight of them both, Jarvis unwavering in his vigil, and McMatters providing companionship, made Bennett feel a surge of gratitude for the strength to be found in their friendships during such trying times. He took a deep breath before approaching them, ready to lend his own support and reassurance as they faced whatever lay ahead together.

"OK, you two. You both look like shit. Go home, get freshened up, and put on clean clothes," said Bennett.
"I don't want her to wake up and not have someone here," said Jarvis.
"I will stay until you're back. I will call you if she wakes."
"Come on, Jarvis, let's get ourselves sorted. We can't help her looking this bad," said McMatters.
"OK. I think I might whiff a bit," admitted Jarvis.

McMatters and Jarvis hurriedly left, their footsteps echoing with a sense of urgency as they navigated the bustling streets.

Jarvis, brimming with determination and excitement, was eager to reach their destination and return in record time. He felt a rush of adrenaline coursing through him, propelling him forward as he envisioned the task ahead. The thrill of the adventure ignited a spark within him, fuelling his desire to accomplish their mission swiftly and efficiently. With each stride they took, the anticipation grew both for what awaited them at their destination and for the satisfaction of knowing they would complete their return journey in no time at all! Bennett had arrived with a stack of paperwork, that had been looming over him like an ominous cloud for far too long. Determined to banish the procrastination that had plagued him, he resolved that while he was here, he would tackle it head-on with unwavering focus and enthusiasm. Armed with a pen in one hand and a steaming cup of coffee in the other, he could already envision the satisfying feeling of crossing each item off his to-do list. It was time to conquer those daunting forms and reports, transforming what once felt like an insurmountable challenge, into a series of manageable tasks that would leave him feeling accomplished and free!

Bennett's thoughts drifted, like a leaf carried by a gentle breeze, to the intricate web of relationships that comprised his social circle. He couldn't help but recognise that his bond with Jarvis and McMatters was deeper and more profound than those he shared with others in the group. These two were not just friends; they were confidants. Allies who had been there through thick and thin, sharing laughter, secrets, and countless memories that created an unshakeable foundation. Then there was Lorraine a newcomer to their ensemble. Although he didn't know her very well yet, Bennett found himself drawn to her genuine spirit and sharp wit. In a remarkably short span of time, he had come to respect her insights and contributions during their recent events, Lorraine was a woman of action, unquestionable action he liked that about her.

This swift admiration was quite unusual for Bennett; he typically took his time assessing new people before forming any judgments or attachments.

However, amidst this tapestry of camaraderie lay a thread of concern: Blythe. Something about Blythe's demeanour had started to unsettle him deeply. The way Blythe interacted with others felt off-kilter, like a discordant note in an otherwise harmonious melody. When the moment felt right, Bennett knew he needed to sit down with Jarvis, McMatters, and Lorraine to share his unease about Blythe's behaviour. He sensed that beneath the surface of jovial gatherings, lay an unsettling truth waiting to be revealed; a mystery that demanded attention, before it could fester further within their circle of friends. For now, he was stepping up to assist Jarvis, by keeping a watchful eye on Katrina, and he couldn't help but feel a surge of excitement about the role he was playing. The thrill of being entrusted with such an important responsibility filled him with energy. As he observed Katrina, her vibrant personality shining through every gesture and laugh, he felt an undeniable connection to the moment. It was like being part of a dynamic dance, where each movement mattered, and his attentiveness would ensure everything went smoothly. With every passing second, he became more aware of how much this experience meant to him, not just as a favour for Jarvis, but as an opportunity to engage with someone so full of life and spirit! Someone he could trust completely; Bennett was loyal to McMatters and Jarvis.

Chapter Ten
McMatters place

McMatters had insisted that Jarvis come over to his place to get freshened up, a request that carried an air of urgency and concern. He was aware of Jarvis's usual struggle with spontaneity, but felt this occasion warranted a little extra effort. After all, Jarvis had a spare suit stashed away at McMatter's residence, specifically for instances just like this event, where appearances mattered more than usual. The suit, neatly hung in the closet, represented not just an article of clothing, but also a lifeline to professionalism and confidence, that Jarvis often found elusive. At that moment, however, Jarvis wasn't in the right frame of mind to refuse; a blend of exhaustion and resignation enveloped him as he recognised the need for change, even if it meant stepping outside his comfort zone. The prospect of donning that suit held the promise of renewal, providing him with an opportunity to shift his mind-set and perhaps rediscover some semblance of clarity amid the chaos swirling around him.

Susan was diligently cleaning in the hallway when, quite unexpectedly, they both stumbled through the door. Their appearance was nothing short of startling; it was as if they had just emerged from a wild encounter with nature, having walked straight through a hedge backwards. Their clothes were dishevelled and tangled, and their hair looked as though it had been tousled by a fierce wind. To add to this chaotic look, there were dark circles under their eyes that hinted at a long night spent sleeping rough on the unforgiving streets. The weariness etched into their faces told stories of discomfort and hardship, contrasting sharply with the serene environment Susan was trying to maintain.

"Morning, Susan. When you're free, could you possibly make us some breakfast please?" Asked McMatters.

"Coming right up. Okay, both of you get in the shower, freshen up, and bring your clothes to me. I'll get them cleaned," said Susan.

"Thanks, Susan."

As the morning sun began to filter through the curtains, casting a warm glow across the kitchen, Susan made her way to prepare breakfast for everyone. The enticing aroma of freshly brewed coffee and sizzling bacon soon filled the air, creating an inviting atmosphere that promised a delightful start to the day. Meanwhile, Jeffery took it upon himself to set the table, carefully arranging each dish and utensil with a sense of purpose and attention to detail. He laid out vibrant plates that caught the light just so, making sure everything was perfect for their meal. In another corner of the house, McMatters retreated to his room, an oasis of solitude, where he indulged in a refreshing shower. The sound of water cascading over him provided a momentary escape from his thoughts, washing away any remnants of weariness from the previous day. Likewise, Jarvis chose to rejuvenate himself in the spare room; as he stepped into the shower's embrace, he savoured these precious moments of tranquillity before joining everyone else for breakfast. Each person was embarking on their own quiet ritual as they prepared to gather and share not only food but also conversation and connection that would nourish their spirits throughout the day.

"Morning, Susan," said Lorraine.
"Miss Lorraine, would you like some breakfast?"
"I could never say no to your breakfast, Susan. Thank you."
Once McMatters and Jarvis felt prepared and ready to embark on their day, they made their way down to the kitchen, where the comforting aroma of freshly brewed coffee wafted through the air. There, they were greeted by Lorraine, who was already setting the stage for a productive morning. Jeffery, with a practiced hand and a warm smile, poured each of them a steaming cup of rich black coffee, its deep colour hinting at its robust flavour and invigorating qualities. Meanwhile, Susan entered the room carrying a delightful spread for breakfast. She carefully balanced plates filled with

golden scrambled eggs, crispy bacon strips, and perfectly toasted bread. The scene was one of camaraderie and warmth, as laughter mingled with the clinking of cutlery, a perfect prelude to what lay ahead in their busy day.

They were all utterly worn out, their bodies heavy with fatigue and their minds clouded from a lack of sleep. Yet, despite their overwhelming exhaustion, they faced a full day ahead that loomed before them like an unyielding mountain. Chief among their priorities was returning to the hospital to see Katrina, whose presence had become a beacon of hope amidst the turmoil. The emotional weight of her situation hung heavily on them, and the urgency to support her through this challenging time propelled them forward, even as weariness tugged at their limbs. Each step they took felt like a battle against gravity itself, but their commitment to be there for Katrina provided the motivation they needed to push through another long day filled with uncertainty and anticipation.

"While I have you both here, we need to chat about Blythe. Not now… but soon," said Lorraine.

"I couldn't agree more," said McMatters.

"If I get my hands on him, I'm not sure anyone will like the consequences. Did you know he hasn't visited Katrina once. His own sister?" said Jarvis.

"As soon as Katrina is awake, I will arrange a meeting with everyone except Blythe," said Lorraine.

"I had the same thoughts. Are you OK covering the club today, Lorraine?" said McMatters.

"Yep. It's all in hand."

Chapter Eleven
Hospital

McMatters and Jarvis arrived at the hospital. Just as they entered the bustling lobby, Jarvis suddenly halted, a look of deep concentration on his face. "Wait a minute!" he declared dramatically, as if he had just discovered the cure for boredom. He dashed off, leaving McMatters standing there with an expression that suggested he was questioning all his life choices. While Jarvis was busy channelling his inner florist, picking out the most vibrant bouquet and debating whether daisies or roses would make a bigger impact, he wanted Katrina to see love and Care when she woken up, McMatters took it upon himself to locate the elusive nurse. He navigated through a maze of impatient patients and overly chatty visitors, feeling somewhat like a contestant on a reality show where the challenge was to find medical staff in record time. The moment Jarvis returned triumphantly with flowers in hand, his grin wider than ever, McMatters appeared back at his side.

"Excuse me, I'm trying to get an update on Katrina Garcia" said McMatters to the nurse.
"Are you a relative?"
"Yes, a brother"
"Her stats have come back up to normal level. I would be expecting her to wake up soon"
"Thank you." McMatters wasn't sure how he managed to get away with saying he was a brother, they did not look alike.

McMatters made his way to the exclusive private room, feeling as though he was entering a VIP section of a celebrity gala. As he stepped inside, he spotted Katrina and Jarvis, who had just arrived at her room and looked as if he had walked off the cover of a fashion magazine. Meanwhile, Bennett was making his grand exit. It was like watching a game of musical chairs, where everyone desperately tried to claim their seat before the music stopped.

"Any change?" asked Jarvis.
"No, a lot of murmured voices, but still sleeping," said Bennett.
"Thank you, for staying Bennett. It means a lot," said Jarvis.
"Don't mention it. Once she's awake, I have something I need to talk to you all about," said Bennett.
"Let me guess… Blythe?" said McMatters.
"Yes, how did you know?" asked Bennett.
"Lorraine just said the same thing, and Jarvis and I were thinking about it too," said McMatters.
"Good to know it's not just me," said Bennett.
"She will ring you to arrange a meeting once Katrina is awake," said Jarvis.
"Sounds good. Speak soon."

Bennett left the room, and as soon as the door clicked shut behind him, Jarvis and McMatters exchanged a glance, that could only be described as a silent conspiracy. They both knew exactly what the other was thinking. Jarvis raised an eyebrow playfully; it was his signature move whenever something absurd happened. McMatters couldn't help but stifle a chuckle. They shared an unspoken bond in that moment, an understanding that transcended words.

"If anyone is to do something to my so-called brother, I want to be the one doing it," whispered Katrina.

Jarvis spun around like a top, his digital eyes wide with surprise.
"Oh, she's awake!" he exclaimed dramatically, as if an earthquake had just hit. Katrina, our little whirlwind of mischief and chaos, had just opened her eyes to greet the day with her signature flair. And what was the first thing out of

her mouth? A request for justice…specifically, she wanted to punish her brother! Clearly, sibling rivalry is alive and well.
"Katrina, I'm so glad you are okay," said Jarvis.
 "Welcome back, Katrina," said McMatters.
"So, the idiot hasn't shown up?" said Katrina.
"No, but don't worry for now. We will sort it out later," said Jarvis.
"I will go grab the nurse and let them know" said McMatters.

While McMatters dashed off in search of a nurse, Jarvis leaned in with the stealth of a cat burglar on a sugar high. He gave Katrina a kiss…oh yes, not just any kiss, but their very first one! It was gentle and sweet, like a perfectly brewed cup of tea on a rainy day. Time seemed to freeze for that fleeting moment; even the clocks appeared to pause in awe, as if witnessing the birth of something magical. Jarvis's heart raced as if it had just run a marathon, while Katrina felt butterflies erupting in her stomach like popcorn in a microwave. Who knew that amidst the chaos of hospital corridors and frantic searches for nurses, love could blossom so unexpectedly?

"I'm so glad you're OK. I was worried," said Jarvis.
"Did you get me the flowers?" asked Katrina.
"Yes."
"They are lovely, thank you."

McMatters returned with a nurse who looked as if she had just had her arm twisted. She stumbled in, clutching her clipboard like a life raft in the middle of an ocean. Armed with an array of monitors and gadgets, the nurse swooped in to check everything. She took some blood and checked Katrina's blood pressure. After her thorough investigation, she delivered the news with seriousness.

"Well, you need to stick around for at least a few hours! If everything checks out okay, you might just get that golden ticket home! But you've got to have someone to keep an eye on you for the next twenty-four hours," said the nurse.

After the nurse left the room, he could practically feel the tension in the air; it was as thick as a bowl of oatmeal. Jarvis and Katrina were clearly gearing up for a conversation that would make a soap opera look like a kindergarten play. Sensing he might be in the way as a third wheel, McMatters decided it would be best to leave. He thought he would go and see Lorraine, since he hadn't seen her properly over the last few days; it had been that chaotic.

Chapter Twelve
Jarvis and Katrina

Jarvis was absolutely over the moon with joy that Katrina was awake and, more importantly, okay. The relief washed over him like a warm wave, as he took in the sight of her blinking eyes and faint smile. However, his heart ached at the painful reminder of the bruises that marred her beautiful face, a stark testament to the ordeal she had faced. Each dark mark told a story of suffering, that he wished he could erase with a mere touch. Yet, amid his sorrow for her pain, there was also an undeniable sense of justice in knowing that those responsible for inflicting such hurt upon Katrina had been made to pay for their actions. It was a bittersweet moment; while he wished she had never experienced such darkness, he felt a surge of gratitude that justice had been served, allowing him to focus on supporting her healing journey ahead.

Jarvis and Katrina had never explicitly discussed the undeniable chemistry that crackled between them, nor had they ever ventured out on a formal date or shared any intimate moments that might have hinted at deeper feelings. Yet, their first kiss was destined to be etched in their memories forever. It was a moment charged with emotion, occurring on the day she finally awoke after enduring her harrowing ordeal. In that instant, with the world around them fading into the background, Katrina felt an overwhelming sense of safety enveloping her once again. The kiss symbolised not just a romantic connection but also a profound promise, one that resonated deeply within Jarvis's heart: nothing would ever threaten her well-being again. He vowed to protect her fiercely and ensure that she would never face such darkness in her life again. He would be her steadfast guardian against any danger that might lurk in the shadows. Their bond was not merely about romance; it was rooted in trust and an unwavering commitment to each other's safety and happiness.

"Katrina, you will come with me once they let you out of here."

"I'd love to."

"I do want to ask, though..." Jarvis took a deep breath, dreading she might say no.

"Yes, Jarvis, yes."

"Really?"

"Yes."

Katrina was undeniably a no-nonsense kind of girl, someone who valued honesty and straightforwardness above all else. Her demeanour exuded a refreshing clarity, that made interactions with her both invigorating and sincere. She had little patience for ambiguity or evasiveness; instead, she preferred to tackle issues head-on, relishing the direct approach in every conversation. With Katrina, there was no beating around the bush, what you saw was what you got. Her candid nature not only fostered trust among her peers, but also encouraged an environment where open dialogue could thrive. In a world often cluttered with indirect communication and hidden meanings, Katrina shone as a beacon of authenticity and forthrightness.

Jarvis was undoubtedly the happiest man in the world, in a tender moment filled with warmth and compassion, he leaned down to kiss Katrina once more, gently and with great care, mindful of her injuries. His lips brushed against hers softly, conveying not just affection but also an overwhelming sense of protectiveness. Each kiss was imbued with an unspoken promise, to cherish her and be her support during this challenging time. The love that blossomed between them was a radiant force, shining brightly even amidst the shadows cast by her struggles.

"Hi Lorraine, can you send your driver please? We are getting out of here," asked Jarvis.

"Yes, I will. He will be there soon," said Lorraine.

Chapter Thirteen
The Club

McMatters and Lorraine were at the club, buried in
paperwork and orders. It was a classic case of work overload,
with documents scattered like an explosion in a stationery
store. They aimed to clear their workload quickly. McMatters
juggled invoices while Lorraine clicked her pen furiously.
Determined to conquer the chaos, everything changed when
Lorraine received a call from Jarvis, as if a switch had been
flipped in her brain.

Suddenly, she was on a mission, channelling her inner
organisational guru with the determination of a cat chasing a
laser pointer. "Right," she thought, rolling up her sleeves as if
preparing for an intense game of whack-a-mole, "it's time to
sort everything out." Her goal? To ensure Jarvis could focus
entirely on looking after Katrina and not do any work. After
all, someone had to help her recover from her recent
adventures. What Lorraine didn't know…but was about to
learn in the most entertaining way possible…was that Jarvis
had slyly instructed the driver to take him and Katrina to the
club instead of his own place. Jarvis entered with a smirk
plastered on his face, supporting Katrina.

"What happened to Katrina resting?" asked Lorraine.
"What can I say," he replied, holding his arms in the air.
"It's my fault," said Katrina.
"Really?" asked Lorraine.
"Yes, we have an issue we need to talk about," said Katrina.
"It could have waited," said McMatters.
Jarvis seized her feet with all the finesse of a seasoned
acrobat and hoisted them onto the sofa. He then nestled a
cushion behind her back, transforming her into the queen of
comfy lounging.

"Would you like a drink, Katrina?" asked Jarvis.
"Please, just a coffee. Black, no sugar. Thanks."

Jarvis whipped up the drink for Katrina and didn't stop there; he also gave her some medicine for the pain.

"OK, my brother. A few issues come to mind. One, the little shit didn't come to see me in the hospital. Oh, and it was Jarvis who came to the rescue and lifted me out of the car. From what I understand, he just stood there, uninterested."

"Well, yes, you could say that, but he didn't really help. Yes, he got in the car, but we all noticed the lack of care when we were searching for you," said Lorraine.

"As a leader, he has to be active. He must jump in. God, if I had a sister, I'd move heaven and earth to find her. He was vacant, which is the best way I can describe what I saw," said McMatters.

"Bennett has asked for a meeting about this, so has Lorraine and McMatters. The question is, are you up for a meeting, Katrina? He's your brother," asked Jarvis.

"Bennett said there was something he couldn't put his finger on, but it bothered him. I agree that he's hiding something," said Lorraine.

"Let's get the meeting done if they are free now. If not, then after we've all had some sleep," said Katrina.

Lorraine called Santos, and McMatters got Bennett on the line. Amazingly, within an hour quicker than you could say "happy hour" they both showed up at the club. It was like they had planned their entrances for maximum drama.

The Meeting

"Welcome Santos and Bennett can I get you anything to drink?" asked McMatters.

"What have you got?" asked Santos.

"Rum, single malt, rum cocktail, or tea and coffee," answered McMatters.

"Tea, two sugars for me," said Santos.

"Coffee, white, one sugar for me," said Bennett. "Katrina, it's nice to see you again. I'm glad this time you're not in the hospital."

"You came to visit?" asked Katrina.

"Yes, I made Jarvis and McMatters take a shower. Talk about a stink!" said Bennett.

Everyone laughed, which helped to relax them after a few days of madness.

"I'm glad you're OK, Katrina," said Santos.

"Thank you very much. I can't express how grateful I am," said Katrina. "I am, though, wanting answers and information on my so-called brother."

"I have put some feelers out. Something doesn't add up, and I hope my hunch is not right this time," said Bennett.

"What's your hunch?"

"I think he was involved in what happened to you, Katrina, like up to his neck in it. I hope I'm wrong, though."

"That's an interesting thought," said Santos. "One of my guys said when you were all scouring the streets, they saw him sitting with the door open in a car, rolling himself a cigarette. He looked calm, which is why my guy told me. He said if it were his sister, he would have been beside himself with worry."

Jarvis and McMatters exchanged glances, a silent understanding passing between them like an unspoken bond. They sensed that Blythe had crossed a line he shouldn't have. Blythe would undoubtedly face the repercussions of his actions, and he would do so in a manner that would be both dramatic and unforgettable.

"One thing I will say though. This isn't the first time he has done stuff like this. I was always the one at risk, and it was usually all about the money. If he is to be punished, it needs to come from me," said Katrina.

"You are not well enough at the moment to dish out punishment," said Jarvis.

"I agree with Jarvis, but I understand Katrina and where she comes from. How about I help Katrina? We all know Blythe fears me," said Lorraine.

"That, I think, will be a good idea. Thank you, Lorraine," said Katrina.

"It will need to be done in front of everyone who helped find you, Katrina. One, so they can see you in action, and two, so they see him punished for being part of it," said Jarvis.

"First, though, we need proof of this. Let's get the message out and gather some info," said McMatters.

"Welcome to the family Katrina," said Bennett.

All raised their cups high, a gesture of warmth and joy, welcoming her into the cherished family. This was more than just a toast; it celebrated love and unity, symbolising their shared bonds. The clinking glasses echoed with laughter, each smile reflecting genuine happiness in embracing her as one of their own. Surrounded by familiar faces and heartfelt sentiments, she felt a profound sense of belonging in the nurturing spirit that defines family.

Chapter Fourteen
Maxine

Maxine was still on cloud nine, her heart fluttering with excitement as thoughts of Demetrio swirled joyfully in her mind. It was as if she had been transported back to her teenage years, filled with innocent crushes and daydreams. Her giddiness was infectious, making her smile uncontrollably as memories of their recent moments together, played like a delightful movie in her head. Each glance and shared laugh sparked a whirlwind of emotions, making her feel alive and vibrant, reminiscent of those carefree days when love was new and thrilling. Maxine revelled in this feeling; it was a sweet reminder of the magic that comes with affection, igniting hope and possibility for the future with someone as charming as Demetrio.

Demetrio was joyfully on his way to Maxine's place, formerly known as Lorraine's home. Ever since Lorraine moved in with McMatters, Maxine embraced this change wholeheartedly, claiming it as her own cosy sanctuary. The thought of his visit filled Maxine with excitement, as she imagined the warm atmosphere and laughter that often filled the air there. It's a place where friendships flourish and cherished memories are made, and he couldn't help but look forward to the delightful conversations and joyful moments that awaited him. They had been getting on like a house on fire, their connection igniting sparks of joy and laughter that lit up every room they entered. Maxine had been counting the days, each one a cherished milestone in their journey together, filled with moments of pure happiness and unforgettable memories. It's hard to believe it had now been eight wonderful months since they first came together, embarking on this beautiful adventure of love. Each day brought new experiences that deepened their bond, from spontaneous outings that turned into delightful escapades, to quiet evenings spent wrapped in each other's company. The joy they shared was palpable, creating an enchanting atmosphere wherever they went, making every moment feel like a celebration of life and love.

Demetrio arrived at the house, and as Maxine opened the door, he revealed a bouquet of flowers.

"Oh, Demetrio, they are wonderful and smell amazing. Come in," she said.

Excitedly, she went to find a vase for the vibrant flowers. Rummaging through her collection, her enthusiasm grew for arranging the blossoms to highlight their dazzling colours. After selecting an elegant glass vase, she admired it before heading to the kitchen. There, with a beaming smile, she brewed rich coffee topped with delicate froth and cocoa. The delightful aroma filled the air, as she prepared to enjoy life's simple pleasures: an exquisite floral arrangement paired with a comforting cup of coffee.

"Let's sit outside Maxine. It's lovely out; we should enjoy it before the weather gets cold."

"Lead the way."

"Maxine, I wanted to talk to you about something. I hope you don't mind, but I need to travel to Italy. A family member is sick and they need help with their restaurant," said Demetrio.

"Oh, I hope they are okay."

"I won't know how ill they are until I get there, but will you come with me?"

Maxine, who was just about to swallow her drink with a delightful smile on her face, suddenly found herself caught off guard. She coughed and spluttered in surprise, causing the refreshing beverage to spill slightly over the edges of her glass.

"I'm sorry, Maxine, I didn't mean to shock you."

"Oh no, no, it's not that. Yes, it was a shock, but I've never been away before. I don't have a passport."

Demetrio laughed. "Don't worry, we can get one sorted. If you would like to come to Italy?"

"Oh yes, that would be wonderful. Oh wow, I'm going on holiday out of the country." Her mind was in a whirlwind.

"Relax, Maxine. Let's finish our drinks and see if we can find everything you need to get a passport sorted. We can get a speed one done the same day, I think," said Demetrio.

"Really, you can get them that fast?"

"Well, from what I know, you can. We would need to plan or book it. I will find out."

"Oooh, we are going on holiday. Well, it's like a holiday."

Maxine was absolutely bursting with excitement at the thought of her upcoming trip to Italy; it seemed like a dreamland filled with elegance, charm, and romance. The idea of wandering through cobblestone streets lined with vibrant cafes, picturesque canals, and historic architecture made her heart race with joy. She envisioned herself sipping espresso in a sun-drenched piazza, while admiring the breathtaking beauty of centuries-old buildings adorned with blooming flowers. Yet, her imagination struggled to paint a clear picture, since she had never ventured beyond her hometown before. This exhilarating prospect was tinged with a hint of apprehension, because she had never set foot on an aeroplane before. The thought of soaring high above the clouds both thrilled and terrified her. What would it feel like to be suspended in the air, witnessing fluffy white clouds drifting serenely beneath her? Would she experience that delightful rush during take-off, or feel nervous as the plane ascended into the vast blue sky? As these thoughts danced around in her mind like playful butterflies, Maxine couldn't help but smile at the adventure that awaited her, both thrilling and daunting, but ultimately filled with promise and wonder.

"Oh my God I need to call Lorraine."

Demetrio chuckled softly, a warm smile spreading across his face as he revelled in the joy Maxine brought into his life. He felt an overwhelming sense of happiness whenever he was with her. Their connection was deep, effortlessly natural, and filled with love. There was something truly enchanting about her exuberance…the way her eyes sparkled with excitement, and how her whole demeanour lit up when she talked about things that fascinated her. It was as if she had a special magic that turned even the simplest moments into vibrant celebrations of life, and Demetrio couldn't help but feel invigorated by her animated spirit. Each laugh they shared seemed to echo through the air, creating a melody of joy that wrapped around them like a warm embrace.

"Lorraine!"
"What's up, Mum?"
"Guess what?"
"Ummm, aliens have invaded?"
"No, silly. I'm going to Italy."
"With Demetrio, I am guessing."
"Yes, a family member of his is sick, so he's going to help with their restaurant and asked me to go with him."
"I hope you said yes."
"I choked, then said yes."
"I'm glad for you, Mum. Have you been away before?"
"No, and I'm scared. We must get a passport. Demetrio said we can get a quick one."
"Yes, it's like fast track. You have to look on the website first and follow the rules so you can do fast track."
"OK, I will check."
"Ring you later, Mum. Got to go, busy bee."
"Bye, Lorraine."

Chapter Fifteen
Katrina

Katrina emerged from her ordeal battered, bruised and swollen. Her face a peculiar tapestry of colours that told a harrowing story of survival. The bruises ranged in hues from deep purples to vivid yellows, each representing a different stage of healing and pain endured. Despite the physical evidence of her struggle, she felt an overwhelming sense of gratitude for being alive. It was a bittersweet realisation; if it hadn't been for Jarvis and his dedicated crew, who had worked tirelessly against the ticking clock of her dwindling oxygen supply, while she was helplessly trapped in the cramped confines of the car boot, locked within a freight container, she might not have made it out at all. Their unwavering determination and quick thinking had quite literally saved her life, leaving her with an immense appreciation for their bravery and selflessness during such a critical moment.

Katrina was far too young to leave this world at the tender age of forty-two. It feels heart-breaking to think of her vibrant life cut short so soon. She had long, dark hair that had a unique texture, kinky and wild, never quite able to be tamed into perfect straightness, yet it also lacked the classic curls one might expect. This distinctive feature added to the richness of her character, and made her more memorable. In her life, Katrina shared a bond with only one brother, Hevran Blythe. Their relationship was a blend of hate and closeness… a complex relationship since they weren't quite full siblings in the traditional sense.

Katrina had a different father from Hevran. From him, she inherited her beautiful golden skin tone, a legacy that connected her to her Mexican heritage, a part of herself she embraced wholeheartedly. Standing tall at six foot one, Katrina often found herself towering over those around her, which sometimes surprised people who met her for the first time.

This height was a trait she inherited from her mother, who was even taller; a family characteristic that made them both stand out in any crowd. Katrina's stature not only gave her a physical presence, but also an undeniable aura of strength and confidence that endeared others to her even more. Not many people could truly handle Katrina. At first glance, she might appear sweet and innocent, with a demeanour that suggests naivety. However, beneath that surface lies a more complex reality. She followed in her brother's footsteps, immersing herself in a world fraught with danger and moral ambiguity; one that most would shy away from, or find simply too challenging to navigate. Whenever her brother found himself in need of assistance, she was right there by his side, ready to help him out despite the risks involved. This willingness to support him speaks volumes about her character. It reveals both her loyalty and her resilience in an environment where few would dare to tread.

With Blythe's recent issues, and a noticeable lack of effective leadership, many things have unfortunately gone awry. However, amidst this turmoil, there has emerged one positive development: the budding relationship between Jarvis and Katrina. Jarvis is someone who truly captured Katrina's attention, and it's not solely since he once came to her rescue in a moment of need. Rather, he possesses an intriguing blend of qualities. He is charming yet devious, caring yet mischievous a quintessential "bad boy" who seems to defy convention in the most alluring ways. This complexity appeals deeply to Katrina, who has always had a soft spot for individuals with a rebellious streak, everyone loves a bad boy! It's this magnetic combination of traits that makes Jarvis not just appealing, but also unforgettable in her eyes. Her brother, however, had revealed his true colours in a way that was both disappointing and disheartening. It became painfully apparent that he cared little for anyone other than himself.

Despite the gravity of the situation and the fact that Katrina could have faced life-threatening circumstances, he never bothered to visit her… not even once… during her time of need. This lack of support has not only hurt Katrina deeply, but also left her feeling abandoned by someone who should have been there for her. She is now determined to confront him about his selfishness and express just how much his actions, or rather lack thereof, have affected her. Conversations with him will not be easy, but she feels it is essential to address these feelings and hold him accountable for his indifference.

Chapter Sixteen
Lorraine

Lorraine found herself deep in thought, reflecting on the recent whirlwind of events that had unfolded around her. It was astonishing to witness how Jarvis and Katrina, once merely acquaintances, had transformed into a couple enveloped in blissful love. The harrowing ordeal of Katrina's kidnapping, which had initially seemed only a tragedy, paradoxically served as the catalyst that brought them closer together. In the wake of such adversity, they discovered a profound connection that blossomed into something beautiful and enduring. Meanwhile, Lorraine's own mother was experiencing a new chapter in her life as well, having fallen head over heels in love with Demetrio. This unexpected romance filled Lorraine with both joy and bittersweet feelings.

Her mother was preparing to embark on her first-ever holiday at the age of fifty-five… a significant milestone that evoked a twinge of sadness for Lorraine. It was hard to reconcile the idea that her mother… who had devoted so much of her life to men of the wrong type… men who had no responsibility other than getting drunk and beating Maxine up… was now embarking on to better things. She had finally found a wonderful man who cherishes her. Maxine was starting to explore love and adventure at this stage in her life. It made Lorraine happy to see this side of her mum. This duality of love blossoming amidst past heartaches, reminded Lorraine of the unpredictable nature of life and relationships; even when it seems like time has passed you by, opportunities for joy can still emerge unexpectedly.

Lorraine was truly in love with McMatters, and now that she had moved in with him, she cherished every moment they spent together. However, lately they hadn't had much quality time due to their busy schedules, and the demands of everyday life. Longing to rekindle their romance and create a special memory together, Lorraine decided it was time for a thoughtful gesture that would sweep McMatters off his feet. It was a beautiful, warm day in September. The sun was shining brightly and temperatures were soaring to a delightful twenty-three degrees Celsius. The gentle breeze carried the sweet scent of blooming flowers, making it the perfect backdrop for an intimate outing. Inspired by the lovely weather, Lorraine envisioned an idyllic picnic where they could escape their routines and enjoy each other's company amidst nature's beauty.

As she contemplated this charming idea, she realised that for her plan to come together seamlessly, they would need a picnic basket filled with delicious treats. However, her memory failed her; she couldn't recall ever seeing one in their home since moving in. Perhaps Susan the House Keeper might have insights on its whereabouts, or even have suggestions about what delightful snacks to include. With excitement bubbling inside her at the thought of spending quality time with McMatters under the warm autumn sun, Lorraine felt determined to make this romantic picnic happen.

"Hi Susan."
"Hello Lorraine, how are you?"
"I'm not bad, thanks. I need some help."
"You name it, I will see what I can do."
"Do you have a picnic basket?"
"Yes, I believe we do. Give me a few minutes, I will see if I can find it for you."
"Thank you, Susan. No rush, I was thinking of Steve and me having a picnic in the garden, maybe for tea."
"That will be nice indeed."
"I will leave you to your harvesting, Susan."
"I will come find you in a bit."
"Thanks again."
"Don't mention it. It's what I am here for."

McMatter's

McMatters was deeply, bone-weary tired. It was a feeling he hadn't experienced in ages, a sensation that had almost become foreign to him over the years. Recent events had taken their toll; the whirlwind of responsibilities and unforeseen challenges meant that sleep had become a rare luxury rather than a nightly routine. Late nights spent wrestling with deadlines and early mornings filled with urgent tasks left little room for rest. As he sat there, he felt the heaviness of his eyelids and a dull ache in his bones, reminding him how much he craved the simple comfort of a good night's sleep…something that now seemed almost out of reach, amidst the chaos surrounding him. In the last four days, he had managed only eighteen hours of sleep, a mere fraction of what his body truly needed to function properly. Despite the exhausting toll this lack of rest was taking, he considered himself fortunate. He had a reliable team around him—dedicated individuals who were more than capable of managing the club and handling any pressing issues in his absence. Their support allowed him to step back when necessary and catch snippets of sleep, knowing he could rely on them to keep everything running smoothly while he fought through the fatigue. He glanced at his phone and saw that Lorraine was calling him.

"Hi Steve."

"Oh, hi Lorraine. Is everything OK?"

"Yes. You sound worn out."

"I am. The tiredness is creeping in."

"Why don't you come home, and I'll make something for tea?"

"That sounds nice. OK, I'll see you soon."

McMatter's place

Lorraine was bubbling with excitement as the day unfolded before her. It was just a picnic, a simple gathering in the sun, but after weeks of chaos and unrelenting demands from work and life, she felt they truly needed this time to reconnect and breathe. The thought of lying on a blanket under the sun's warm embrace filled her with joy. Although Lorraine still wasn't feeling fantastic generally, she considered herself okay. She had become increasingly aware of a persistent fatigue that clung to her like an unwelcome shadow. It was perplexing; she couldn't pinpoint why she felt so off-kilter, and this mystery was driving her a bit crazy. However, it was such a beautiful day that Lorraine decided to make the most of it. She envisioned herself and McMatters enjoying an idyllic picnic in their expansive garden, a space so large one could easily get lost within its verdant corners and hidden nooks.

Earlier that day, during her leisurely stroll around the garden, Lorraine had stumbled upon an enchanting old archway entwined with climbing vines leading to a quaint gate. With curiosity sparkling in her eyes, she pushed open the gate and stepped into a vast open area reminiscent of a wild meadow bursting with life, a perfect spot for their romantic escape beneath an endless blue sky sprinkled with fluffy clouds. The allure of such an enchanting setting filled Lorraine's heart with anticipation, as she envisioned blankets spread over lush grass, delicious treats laid out before them, laughter mingling with the gentle whispers of nature surrounding them.
Susan helped Lorraine, who was bubbling with excitement, prepare for the delightful picnic she had been dreaming about. Together, they gathered an array of delicious treats, starting with a lovely bottle of crisp white wine that would sparkle in the sunlight. The vibrant red grapes added a pop of colour to their spread, while the gorgeous green salad was perfectly fresh and inviting for Steve. They carefully arranged an assortment of sandwiches, each one brimming with flavour, alongside creamy cheese paired with crunchy crackers for a satisfying snack. As if that weren't enough to tantalise their taste buds, they included mini cocktail sausages and savoury sausage rolls, perfect finger foods that would surely be a hit!

To top it all off, Susan had prepared one large slice of decadent chocolate cake, rich and indulgent, which they could share using two spoons…a sweet gesture meant to embody their joyful celebration together. With napkins neatly folded and glasses set aside for their refreshing drinks, everything was packed up beautifully and ready to greet Steve when he arrived home.

The anticipation in the air was palpable as they looked forward to enjoying this wonderful outdoor feast together! Steve walked through the door, and as he did, his eyes lit up with joy upon seeing Lorraine waiting for him. Her warm smile radiated happiness, instantly brightening his day. It was a delightful sight that filled his heart with warmth; the mere thought of having someone special at home still felt like a wonderful novelty. This new chapter in his life brought an exhilarating sense of companionship and comfort that he had longed for. Each time he walked into their shared space and found her there, it filled him with gratitude and excitement, reminding him how lovely it was to come home to someone who cared deeply for him. He greeted Lorraine with a kiss.

"Hungry?" asked Lorraine.
"Starving."
"Good, follow me," said Lorraine.

Steve chuckled heartily at the delightful memory, a warm smile spreading across his face as he recalled the enchanting moment when they first crossed paths. It was a time filled with excitement and nervous anticipation, and he distinctly remembered saying those charming words to Lorraine on more than one occasion. Each time, it felt as if they were weaving a special thread into the fabric of their budding relationship, each chuckle echoing with promise and laughter that would bind them together. The joy of the recollection danced in his heart, reminding him of how far they had come since that serendipitous introduction.

Chapter Seventeen
Maxine and Demetrio

Maxine was absolutely buzzing with excitement, her heart racing with an energy she could hardly contain. The thought of embarking on a journey with Demetrio, leaving the country together, sent waves of exhilaration coursing through her veins. It felt as if she were living in a fairy-tale, where every moment sparkled with the promise of adventure and new experiences. This opportunity was not just an ordinary trip; it was like a dream, Maxine and Demetrio were buzzing with excitement as they set off to the passport office, eager to secure Maxine's very first passport. This was not just any trip; it marked the beginning of an incredible adventure that would take them to the enchanting landscapes of Italy! However, upon arriving at the office, they discovered that obtaining the passport on the same day would require an additional fee. While this news initially caused a slight pang of apprehension, Maxine quickly weighed it against the thrill of being able to leave for Italy as soon as the perfect flight opportunity came up.

Yet beneath her excitement, lay a swirling mix of emotions. Maxine had never flown before. Correction: she had never even stepped foot outside her home country! The prospect of boarding an airplane and soaring through the skies, filled her with both wonder and trepidation. Countless thoughts raced through her mind like a whirlwind: What would it feel like to be thousands of feet in the air? How would she navigate a foreign land where everything from street signs to menus might be in a different language? The unknown loomed large, transforming what should have been pure joy, into a cocktail of exhilaration and anxiety. As they stood in line at the passport office, Maxine couldn't help but feel overwhelmed by these questions and uncertainties.

Yet, amidst all this fear of what lay ahead, there was also a glimmering hope a promise of adventure and discovery, that awaited them across oceans and borders. It was this tantalising vision that ultimately fuelled her courage, pushing her to embrace both the thrill and anxiety that travel inevitably brings. A dream come true, a magical escape from the mundane that she had longed for. She could already envision exploring vibrant new landscapes side by side with Demetrio, sharing laughter and creating memories that would last a lifetime. Maxine just didn't know what to expect which made it scary. They stood in the queue waiting. It was a long, long line.

Chapter Eighteen
Jarvis and Katrina

Upon leaving the pulsating atmosphere of Dreams Night
Club, Jarvis took Katrina back to his place with a sense of
purpose and determination. He wanted to ensure her well-
being and help her heal, both physically and emotionally. As
he carefully treated her cuts and bruises, his gentle touch
conveyed not only a desire to alleviate her pain, but also an
earnest commitment to nurturing her recovery. Jarvis went
above and beyond in his efforts; he prepared breakfast in bed
for Katrina, presenting a delightful spread that included fresh
fruit, warm pastries, and steaming coffee, each bite crafted
with care. In the evenings, he arranged sumptuous meals from
Demetrio's, a renowned restaurant owned by Demetrio, a
close friend, known for its exquisite cuisine. The soft clinking
of cutlery against fine China accompanied their intimate
dinners by candlelight, where they could engage in heart-
warming conversations and share peals of laughter.
Through these thoughtful gestures of wining and dining her
with elegance and charm, Jarvis aimed not only to satisfy
Katrina's physical needs, but also to convey a deeper
message: that she was truly special. In each carefully planned
moment together, whether over breakfast or beneath the soft
glow of dinner candles, Jarvis sought to create an atmosphere
where Katrina could feel cherished and valued…a sanctuary
away from the world, that had been harsh on her spirit.

Jarvis had always prided himself on being a true gentleman,
and considering Katrina's recent ordeal, he was determined to
respect her boundaries. He refrained from making any
romantic advances, fully aware that she was still recovering
from the physical and emotional pains inflicted by the brutal
beating she had endured. Yet tonight was different; it marked
a moment where he could shift his focus entirely to treating
her with the care and affection she truly deserved. He wanted
to help her forget, even if just for a little while, the trauma

that had weighed heavily on her spirit. With this intention, Jarvis set out to create an enchanting atmosphere, that would envelop Katrina in warmth and comfort. He meticulously prepared every detail of the evening with love and thoughtfulness.

The hot tub was ready…a serene oasis filled with bubbling water that promised relaxation, and he adorned the surrounding area with fragrant aromatherapy candles, flickering gently in anticipation of their special night together. Delicate flowers were artfully arranged nearby, adding splashes of colour and delightful scents that would further enhance the ambiance. Aware that he hadn't engaged in such intimate settings for over seven years, Jarvis sought guidance from Susan, who specialised in creating memorable experiences for couples. Her expertise proved invaluable; she patiently explained each element Jarvis should include to craft an unforgettable romantic evening. From choosing the right flowers to understanding how to arrange them effectively, everything mattered when setting up a night meant for connection and healing. The culmination of his efforts included scattering soft petals across their bed…a pathway leading towards an inviting scene of indulgence, featuring champagne chilling on ice alongside luscious strawberries dipped in rich chocolate. Each item was thoughtfully selected, not only for its visual appeal, but also for its ability to evoke romance and pleasure.
Jarvis envisioned leading Katrina into this intimate space, blindfolded so as not to reveal too much before unveiling his carefully curated surprise. Jarvis imagined her reaction as they approached the hot tub, her curiosity piqued by sensory anticipation, allowing her heart rate to slow as she surrendered herself completely into this cocoon of care he had crafted just for her sake. In his mind's eye, this night would be a turning point: one where joy could begin again, after so much heartache had shadowed their lives. He was all set and now waiting until after the evening meal.

Chapter Nineteen
Passport Office

After Maxine and Demetrio had endured a long, gruelling four-hour wait in the never-ending queue to get their passports, they finally found themselves in the processing area, where the joy of waiting continued unabated. Maxine's feet were protesting like they had just run a marathon, though let's be honest, the only thing they'd sprinted towards was a seat that never materialised. At this point, she was so desperate for relief that every few minutes she lifted one foot off the ground like it was a hot potato, and began circling her ankles with all the grace of a flamingo trying to do ballet.

 If anyone were to look closely, they might think she was practicing some sort of interpretive dance called "The Frustrated Traveller." Meanwhile, Demetrio eyed his watch with growing impatience, wondering if he should start taking bets on how long it would take before they could finally escape this bureaucratic circus.

Demetrio generally was feeling OK; a little pain in his lower back from staying in one place for too long. Demetrio felt like a statue, he was pretty sure he could hear birds nesting on his head. But his mind was racing with concern for Maxine. It baffled him why there were no benches or chairs in sight, especially when people were clearly in desperate need of a rest! I mean, after standing around like they were auditioning for a role as human traffic cones, wouldn't it be nice to plop down somewhere? He glanced back at the queue they had just escaped from, and let out a sigh of relief that echoed louder than the most dramatic soap opera scene. That line had seemed to stretch on forever, twisting and turning like an endless roller coaster, except without any of the fun! He felt as if he might have aged twenty years while waiting; in fact, he wouldn't be surprised if someone mistook him for an ancient tree stump by now. Each minute spent there was akin to running a marathon with only one shoe on, exhausting and utterly ridiculous! Now free from that torturous snaking line,

Demetrio couldn't help but appreciate his newfound liberation from what felt like the world's slowest-moving queue.

Demetrio stood there, tapping his foot impatiently, pondering just how long this queue was going to take. "Processing," they called it, but really it felt more like a game of musical chairs where the music had stopped and no one was moving. He imagined the clerks behind the desk squinting at screens and muttering to themselves, while checking credentials as if they were deciphering ancient hieroglyphics. I mean, seriously, is anyone truly who they say they are these days? With all the identity swaps happening out there, who's to say that guy in front of him wasn't an undercover alien trying to assimilate into human society? Demetrio chuckled at the thought; perhaps he should start carrying around a tinfoil hat just in case!

Chapter Twenty
Blindfold

Katrina had just savoured the most exquisite meal from Demetrio's restaurant, a hidden gem that never failed to impress with its culinary delights. The flavours danced on her palate, each bite a harmonious blend of spices and ingredients meticulously crafted by the talented chefs. This place truly is remarkable; it consistently delivers an unforgettable dining experience that lingers in the memory long after the last morsel has been consumed. Although Demetrio's typically does not offer takeaway services. Due to the close friendship between McMatters and Jarvis with Demetrio himself, along with Lorraine's mother dating him, Katrina found herself benefiting from a unique arrangement.

This special connection allowed them access to exclusive services that most patrons could only dream of receiving. Katrina felt immensely grateful for this opportunity; it was not just about enjoying delicious food, but also about sharing in a sense of community and connection, that made the experience even more meaningful. Each meal became a celebration of friendships and relationships, enhancing her appreciation for both the cuisine and those who prepared it. With Katrina refraining from stepping outside during this turbulent time, the cuts and bruises that mar her skin are still a vivid testament to her recent struggles, showcasing a kaleidoscope of colours that tell their own stories of pain and resilience. Each mark is like a brushstroke on a canvas, blending shades of purple, yellow, and green, the remnants of an unseen battle that she wishes to keep hidden from the world.

Overwhelmed by self-consciousness and the fear of judgment, Katrina feels an aversion to being seen in such a vulnerable state. In this period of retreat, Jarvis has taken it upon himself to care for her within the confines of his home, an abode that can only be described as a luxurious man-pad.

This space is adorned with modern decor and plush furnishings, offering both comfort and style.

It serves as a sanctuary where he hopes Katrina can find solace amid her turmoil. Here, surrounded by sleek lines and soft lighting, Jarvis strives to create an atmosphere that fosters healing. A stark contrast to the chaos outside. His attentiveness reflects not just his concern for her physical well-being, but also his desire to provide emotional support during this challenging chapter in her life.

"OK, Katrina, I have something special for you, but I need you to put on the blindfold so you don't see part two of my surprise," said Jarvis.

"Well, OK… I guess I trust you," she said, smiling.

Jarvis carefully placed a soft satin blindfold over Katrina's eyes, ensuring it was snug enough to maintain the element of surprise he had meticulously planned. He was cautious not to make it too tight, avoiding discomfort or the risk of it slipping off. Holding her hand gently, Jarvis guided Katrina up the stairs, his touch reassuring and warm. As they ascended, Katrina felt an unusual sensation underfoot; the surface beneath her toes seemed to shift slightly with each step. This intriguing feeling soon gave way to the unmistakable chill of tiles against her feet, and she realised they must be in the bathroom. Jarvis then gently sat Katrina on a sturdy surface and placed a comforting hand on her shoulder.

In a playful motion, he swung her legs up and around, causing Katrina to squeal in surprise and delight, a sound that echoed with excitement. In that moment, all apprehensions melted away as laughter filled the air, transforming a potentially tense experience into one brimming with joy and anticipation. Jarvis gently undid the ties of Katrina's robe, allowing the soft fabric to cascade down her shoulders and slide off her body. As the garment fell, it made a soft thud on the floor, creating a momentary stillness around them. Katrina's bare feet found now themselves on a rough, bumpy surface, reminiscent of stepping onto tiny pebbles or a sandy beach.

Despite this unusual sensation, she was pleasantly surprised to find it wasn't cold. In fact, the room's atmosphere enveloped her in a warm embrace that felt soothing and relaxing. The combination of textures and temperatures created an intimate atmosphere, heightening her awareness of every detail around her.

Chapter Twenty-One
Picnic

McMatters' curiosity was piqued as he followed Lorraine into the vibrant garden, her laughter echoing like sweet music in the air. To his surprise, she began skipping joyfully across the lush green grass, her carefree spirit infectious and delightful to witness. McMatters couldn't help but smile at the sight of Lorraine radiating happiness and contentment, as if the garden was a magical place that filled her with pure joy. As he continued to follow her light-hearted dance through the colourful flowers and buzzing bees, he wondered what whimsical adventure Lorraine had in mind. The sun beamed down brightly from above, casting warm rays that enveloped them in a golden glow. Feeling a bit overheated from both excitement and warmth, McMatters decided to take off his jacket. He tossed it casually over one shoulder while loosening his tie, then unbuttoning the top button of his shirt for comfort, it really was a hot day!

With each step he took behind Lorraine, he felt more drawn into her joyful world, eager to share in whatever delightful escapade awaited them in this enchanting garden. McMatters was overflowing with joy and felt incredibly fortunate to have found someone as remarkable as Lorraine. It never ceased to amuse him how there seemed to be absolutely nothing she couldn't tackle or transform into something extraordinary. Whether it was a challenging project at work, a spontaneous adventure, or even a drastic action, Lorraine approached everything with infectious enthusiasm. She didn't hesitate for a moment; instead, she dove in headfirst, embracing every opportunity with an open heart and a fearless spirit. Her zest for life turned even the most mundane tasks into exciting escapades, leaving everyone around her inspired and uplifted by her boundless energy and unwavering confidence.

McMatters finally caught up with Lorraine as he reached the gate to the meadow, a threshold he hadn't crossed since he first bought the house. A whole five years had slipped by! As he stepped through that familiar archway, a delightful rush of colour enveloped him; wildflowers painted the landscape in vibrant hues, creating a breath-taking tapestry of nature's artistry. Each bloom seemed to dance joyfully in the gentle breeze, their petals fluttering like confetti at a celebration. The air was filled with an enchanting fragrance that was simply wonderful, evoking memories of sunlit afternoons and numerous carefree days spent outdoors.

It felt as if the meadow itself was welcoming him back with open arms, inviting him to bask in its beauty and embrace the joy that came with reconnecting to this hidden gem. As he looked around, a sudden wave of realisation washed over him: Lorraine had vanished! A slight panic began to creep into his chest, each heartbeat echoing the urgency of the moment. He glanced down and noticed tiny marks tracing through the tall grasses, where vibrant wildflowers danced in the gentle breeze. Their bright colours seemed to mock his increasing worry as they swayed playfully under the sun. Despite his frantic searching, he couldn't discern where else she might have gone; it was as if she had simply melted away into thin air, leaving only whispers of her presence behind. The beauty of the landscape contrasted sharply with his growing unease, creating a surreal atmosphere, that both enchanted and frightened him. McMatters followed the tiny, whimsical impressions left in the soft wild grass, a trail that led him to a delightful clearing bathed in dappled sunlight. There, he discovered Lorraine, who had thoughtfully arranged a charming picnic setup, complete with a vibrant blanket and an inviting basket brimming with delectable treats.

As he approached, he noticed her gracefully holding two glasses of wine aloft, glasses filled with rich, ruby-red liquid that caught the light just right. He realised with an amused smile that this was no ordinary wine; it was oddly different he knew the flavour well but couldn't think of when he last tasted it. Lorraine truly had an appreciation for the finer things in life, and her penchant for luxury made moments like these feel even more special and joyful. The air was filled with laughter and warmth as they prepared to enjoy their leisurely afternoon together amidst nature's beauty.

Chapter Twenty-Two
Exhausted

Maxine was on the brink of collapse; her body weary and aching from the relentless strain of their ordeal. Demetrio, her steadfast companion, was fading fast beside her, his strength waning as exhaustion seeped into his bones. Yet in that moment of desperation and fatigue, a spark of hope flickered between them: they finally had Maxine's passport firmly in her grasp. It felt like a tangible lifeline amidst their overwhelming struggles. If only they hadn't been consumed by so much pain and fatigue, they might have found the energy to leap for joy, to celebrate this small but significant victory that could change everything for them. Instead, they held onto the document with a mix of relief and disbelief, knowing that it represented not just identification, but also the promise of freedom from their current plight.

"I never want to do that again," said Maxine.
"It's OK. It's ten years before it will need renewal," said Demetrio.
"Please tell me we won't have to come back here to do a renewal."
"No, we can do that by post or online. If I can figure out how to operate the website."
"Phew. I am so hungry." She sighed.
"Let's go and get some real food."
"I need to pack as well, when is the flight?"
"Tomorrow morning at six o'clock."
"Oh, that's early. So, we just turn up at six and get on the plane?"
Demetrio chuckled, amused by the fact that Maxine had never been to an airport. He imagined her wide-eyed wonder navigating bustling terminals, surrounded by diverse travellers with their own stories. He remembered his own airport experiences. The aroma of coffee and pastries, rhythmic announcements, and the anticipation in the air, as

people awaited flights to distant destinations. How could someone miss such vibrant activity?

"Not quite. We have to check in at three a.m. and drop off our bags."
"You mean my bags don't come with me?"
"They go into the luggage hold under the plane. We sit above and can take one bag with us each, so we need to choose wisely what to put in the bag."
"Did you say three in the morning?"
"Yes."
"When do we sleep?"
"On the plane. Most people sleep."

Demetrio could see that Maxine was deeply engaged in processing all the information he had shared with her. Her brow furrowed slightly, a tell-tale sign of concentration as she absorbed each detail. It was indeed a substantial amount for someone whose first flight experience had only begun at the tender age of fifty-five… a milestone that many take for granted at a much younger age. For Maxine, this journey into the skies represented not just an adventure, but also a significant step into a world filled with new experiences and challenges, making her efforts to grasp every facet of flying even more commendable.

Chapter Twenty-Three
Petals

Katrina found herself perched precariously on the edge of an unforgiving surface, the hardness beneath her contrasting sharply with the vulnerability she felt at that moment. Her bare skin was exposed to the cool air surrounding her, sending shivers down her spine as she grappled with her surroundings. The ground below her feet was not smooth; instead, it greeted her with a sensation that was both bumpy and bobbly, like a sea of unyielding pebbles that seemed to shift beneath her feet. In this state of undress, she wore nothing but a blindfold, which shrouded her vision and plunged her into darkness, heightening all, of her other senses. Sounds became amplified, the rustle of fabric somewhere in the distance perhaps, or the soft murmur of whispers that danced around her like fleeting shadows. Each breath she took felt electric with anticipation as she sat there, caught between fear and excitement, craving to discover what lay beyond the veil covering her eyes.

Jarvis gently guided her to adjust her seating position, encouraging her to lower herself down until she found herself perched upon a surprisingly smooth surface. One that felt almost like a plush cushion beneath her. As Katrina settled in, an overwhelming sense of curiosity washed over her; she had no idea where she was or what to expect next. In that moment of uncertainty, Jarvis activated something and suddenly, water surged towards her feet with an exhilarating rush. The liquid swirled around her rapidly, bubbling with life and energy as it danced against her skin. The sensations were peculiar yet undeniably pleasant. A delightful juxtaposition of warmth and coolness that enveloped her with its gentle embrace. It was both invigorating and soothing at the same time, washing away any lingering apprehensions as she surrendered to the experience, feeling utterly relaxed amidst the playful chaos of swirling water.

Jarvis stood transfixed; his gaze unwavering as he watched Katrina immerse herself in the experience unfolding before her. Every subtle detail captured his attention. The way she reacted to the sensations, the caress of different textures that danced against her skin. He could almost feel the contrast between the hard surfaces and soft materials as they brushed against her, each touch igniting a spark of curiosity and delight in her eyes. As water cascaded down her body and kissed her toes, swirling playfully around her feet, he noticed an unmistakable joy radiating from her expression. A mixture of surprise and exhilaration, that lit up her face like a sunrise breaking through a cloudy sky.

The gentle lapping of the water seemed to invigorate not just her senses, but also stirred something deep within him, a shared connection in this moment of blissful discovery. It was clear that this delightful surprise was enchanting for Katrina; she was savouring every second, as if it were an exquisite gift meant solely for her enjoyment.

Jarvis couldn't help but notice the mesmerising ripples of water, as they began to bubble around Katrina. The once warm and inviting liquid, now creeping slowly around her ankles, was becoming a stark reminder of the cooling air that surrounded them, wrapping its invisible fingers around their skin. He could feel the tension in the atmosphere shift, a blend of anticipation and excitement setting his heart racing. Kneeling on the floor, he felt an exhilarating rush; he knew he had a precious moment to indulge in playful intimacy. With tender care, he gently pulled Katrina's lower body closer to the edge of the seat, ensuring she felt both secure and cherished in that fleeting moment. As if orchestrating a delicate dance, Jarvis lifted each leg onto his shoulders with reverence and intention, creating an intimate connection that thrummed with unspoken desire.

It was as if time itself had slowed down just for them, enveloping them in a cocoon of warmth that contrasted beautifully with the coolness surrounding them. Jarvis then placed his tongue with exquisite tenderness; a playful gesture designed to tease and tantalise Katrina. As the water began to rise, creeping up towards her waist, he skilfully harnessed its buoyancy to amplify her sensations. The gentle caress of the water played beautifully with the bubbles that swirled around her most sensitive areas, creating a delightful symphony of sensations that danced across her skin. Each movement was deliberate and infused with a sense of mischief, as if he were conducting an intimate orchestra where every note was meant to heighten their shared experience.

Chapter Twenty-Four
Wildflowers

McMatters joined Lorraine on the picnic blanket, which was spread out invitingly in the heart of a vibrant wild meadow, that was bursting with an explosion of colourful flowers swaying gently in the warm breeze. As he took a moment to breathe in the delightful fragrance of the blooming wildflowers which surrounded them, he picked up a glass of wine, its rich crimson hue glistening in the sunlight. With a soft smile, he leaned closer and kissed Lorraine tenderly, feeling an overwhelming rush of joy and affection wash over him. In that instant, he realised just how much he had truly missed her presence. More than words could express or even than he had initially understood. The warmth of their connection felt electric amidst nature's beauty, and it was as if time itself paused to celebrate their reunion.

"Let's eat," said Lorraine.
As Lorraine eagerly unpacked the picnic basket, McMatters couldn't help, but be pleasantly surprised at how beautifully arranged everything looked. The vibrant colours of the food choices made his mouth water, and his stomach rumbled in anticipation; after all, he was absolutely starving. He started with some delightful Swiss-style sandwiches stuffed with savoury ham, creamy cheese, fresh salad, and a dollop of mayonnaise, that performed a dance on his palate. Each bite was a burst of flavour that ignited his taste buds, beckoning him to try more. Next, he added a tuna and cucumber sandwich to his plate. One that offered a refreshing contrast to the richness of the earlier bites.
The combination was delightful! He then indulged in some playful cocktail sausages and flaky sausage rolls, a classic picnic treats before finishing off with a perfectly boiled egg, that added an extra protein punch to his meal. As they both settled down for this delicious feast under the open sky, he poured another glass of wine for them to share. However, as

72

he took a sip, he found himself puzzled by its unique taste; it had an intriguing flavour profile that lingered on his tongue, yet felt oddly familiar, though he couldn't quite put his finger on why it tasted different than usual.

This curious sensation stirred something within him, but didn't distract him from enjoying the moment.

To keep things light-hearted and fun at their picnic gathering, McMatters playfully fed Lorraine some juicy grapes while they shared bites of rich chocolate cake together. Each morsel melted in their mouths like pure bliss as they washed it down with yet more wine. Yet amidst this blissful atmosphere filled with laughter and chatter about their day so far, McMatters felt an unusual breeze wafting through the air, a subtle shift that tugged at his senses without revealing its source. His attention was drawn back to Lorraine when he noticed something odd: she had covered up the wine label with another blank label. This small act baffled him; questions swirled in his mind about why she would go through such trouble to obscure it. Instead of voicing his curiosity right away about both the wine's peculiar taste and her mysterious labelling choice, McMatters decided to wait patiently and see if she would eventually offer up any information about it herself. It turned into a game of sorts, a dance between inquisitiveness and anticipation, leaving him eager for whatever revelations might come next during their lovely picnic outing together.

Lorraine gently pushed the basket aside, creating a little space for herself as she leaned in closer. With a playful glint in her eye, she began to unbutton his shirt, each button releasing a soft whisper of fabric that heightened the moment's intimacy. As her lips met his, a spark ignited between them, sending delightful shivers down their spines. She continued her exploration by trailing kisses from his lips to the tender curve of his neck, savouring each moment with deliberate slowness. Her warm breath danced across his skin as she descended further down his chest, creating an intoxicating blend of passion and anticipation. "This is the life," thought McMatters to himself, feeling utterly captivated by the blissful experience unfolding before him. The world outside faded away, leaving just the two of them enveloped in this enchanting moment. With each gentle kiss and caress, he couldn't help but think how easily he could get used to this exquisite connection, this spellbinding dance of affection that felt both thrilling and profoundly satisfying.

Chapter Twenty-Five
Bubbles

As the shimmering water swirled and crested up to Katrina's waist, a sense of exhilaration enveloped them both. Jarvis gently placed her legs back down into the inviting depths, his heart racing with anticipation. He leaned in closer, capturing Katrina's lips in a tender kiss, that ignited sparks of passion between them. It was as if time itself had paused, allowing them to savour every fleeting moment. As their mouths moved together in an intoxicating dance, his hand wandered with deliberate slowness, continuing the playful teasing that had become their intimate language. He slid his fingers around the delicate edge of her form, gliding up and down with tantalising care.

The water splashed softly around them, creating a backdrop of soothing sounds, that mingled with the soft symphony of their breathing. Every now and then, he would hear a soft moan escape from Katrina's lips, a sound so sweet it felt like music to his ears. Each sound filled him with an intoxicating thrill. It urged him onwards as he explored this beautiful connection they shared in that enchanting moment by the water's edge. Jarvis and Katrina had never experienced an intimate moment together; their relationship, though filled with affection, had only ever included the gentle brush of lips in a fleeting kiss. Yet in that simplicity lay the potential for something profound. Jarvis longed to create a memory for Katrina. One that would be etched into her mind and heart, a vivid chapter in the story of their love that she would cherish forever. He envisioned a scene imbued with romance and tenderness, where every detail was meticulously crafted to ensure it became an unforgettable experience. With each passing day, his anticipation grew, as he dreamed of sweeping her off her feet in a way that transcended their previous encounters, taking them both to new heights of connection and emotional depth.

Jarvis pulled away, his heart racing with excitement, and gently positioned Katrina on the smooth seat beside him. The atmosphere was electric, filled with a sense of intimacy that hung in the air like sweet perfume. He handed her a delicate glass of champagne, the golden liquid sparkling like captured sunlight. As they shared luscious strawberries, each one lovingly dipped in the effervescent champagne, their laughter danced together like bubbles rising in a glass. The taste was an explosion of sweet and tart flavours, perfectly complemented by the crispness of the bubbly drink. Jarvis turned up the jets on the Jacuzzi, softly bubbles danced around her delicate parts, bubbles tickled down below. Katrina's joyful laughter rang out like chimes on a breezy day, her happiness infectious as they savoured each decadent bite together under a canopy of imaginary stars, that only they were able to appreciate.

Katrina found herself engulfed in a whirlwind of sensory overload, even though her eyes remained shrouded by the blindfold. The playful and tantalising touch of Jarvis sent electric currents racing through her body, igniting a fire within her that she could barely contain. Each brush of his fingers stirred her senses, awakening emotions that had lain dormant for far too long. The effervescent bubbles of champagne danced around her mouth, their delicate fizz mingling with the sweet aroma of ripe strawberries, creating an intoxicating symphony that wrapped around her taste buds with a warm embrace. In this moment suspended in time, every sensation felt amplified; it was as though the world had narrowed down to just the two of them.

With each burst of flavour and texture, everything inside her seemed to explode, like vibrant fireworks lighting up the night sky. Her longing for Jarvis grew stronger with every heartbeat; she craved his presence and connection with an intensity that left her breathless. All she wanted was to be close to Jarvis, to feel him completely, body and soul, lost in their shared passion amidst this delightful chaos.

Chapter Twenty-Six
Rolling around

Lorraine had opened Steve's shirt, revealing the enticing contours of his chest. With a playful glint in her eye, she teased his nipples, her fingers lightly dancing over his skin, sending shivers down his spine. The atmosphere was charged with electric intimacy, as she shifted her focus to his trousers. With deft movements, she gently loosened them, ensuring the fabric no longer constricted him. This action not only provided him with the freedom to breathe, but also heightened the tension and anticipation between them. Each moment was filled with palpable energy, deepening their connection in ways words could barely capture.

Steve, despite his internal conflict about taking away all the fun, found himself irresistibly drawn to glide his hand up Lorraine's dress. The thrill of the moment electrified the air around them, as if every heartbeat echoed their unspoken desires. He didn't need to wrestle with the dress; it fit her so loosely, it was as if it had been especially designed for just this encounter. It was almost as though Lorraine had orchestrated this scenario with care, knowing each touch would ignite a spark between them. This blend of spontaneity and intention made his heart race faster, deepening his appreciation for how naturally everything unfolded in that moment.

Steve felt a surge of exhilaration as he realised his suspicions were correct: Lorraine was not wearing any undergarments. This revelation ignited a playful spark within him, providing the perfect opportunity to tease her. The atmosphere crackled with excitement as Steve leaned into the moment, his mischievous grin hinting at the fun that was about to unfold. As he found that sweet spot, Lorraine's response was immediate and electrifying; she let out a delightful moan that filled the air. Steve seized this moment of connection; with his other hand, he pulled Lorraine close, drawing her into a fervent kiss, that conveyed all the passion simmering between them.

It was a kiss filled with unspoken words and shared secrets, a beautiful culmination of teasing and desire. While rolling in the vibrant, sun-kissed wildflower meadow, they shed their clothing like petals, yearning to remove every obstruction between them and the ecstasy of their shared moment. The air was thick with the fragrance of blooming flowers, enveloping them as they laughed and tumbled through a tapestry of colour. Each discarded thread of fabric symbolised their desire to connect more deeply, to feel the warmth of skin against skin.

In this idyllic sanctuary, amidst nature's beauty, they embraced each other and the exhilarating freedom of being entirely vulnerable in a world bursting with life. They made love, a beautiful expression of intimacy, as sweet and pure as the sun's golden rays that enveloped them.

Each moment was a delicate dance of connection, satisfying one another's deepest desires through an exquisite exchange of sensations. With every caress, their skin tingled, igniting a fire within. The world around them faded, as they lost themselves in this union, where time stood still. They explored each other with gentle curiosity, discovering new heights of ecstasy that left them breathless.

After dressing, they lay together on the soft grass, gazing up at the vast sky. The sun, a fiery orb, began its slow descent, casting a warm glow. As night approached, the air grew cooler and tranquil. Together, they felt as if time had paused; their hearts beat in unison while the first stars twinkled like diamonds. It was a moment suspended between day and night, a fleeting yet timeless connection, that spoke volumes without words.

Chapter Twenty-Seven
Good things come to those who wait

Jarvis, feeling a surge of confidence, decided that he had Katrina right where he wanted her. The playful atmosphere between them was electric, charged with unspoken tension and undeniable chemistry. With a mischievous grin, he realised it was time to make a move, before they both turned into prunes in the warm embrace of the hot tub's bubbling waters. As he let the water drain away, the soothing jets fell silent, and the steam began to dissipate into the cool evening air. Jarvis then reached for Katrina's legs with a gentle yet purposeful touch, spinning her around as if they were caught in a delightful dance. The moment felt suspended in time; his heart raced at the intimacy of their shared laughter and playful banter. With careful hands, he helped her stand up, then step out of the hot tub, their skin glistening with droplets of water under the soft glow of ambient lights, that surrounded them.
The world outside faded away as they shared this exhilarating instant, a blend of warmth from both the hot tub and their connection, that left them breathless and craving further adventure together.

They were now in a close embrace. Jarvis kissed her tenderly at first, his lips brushing against hers with a gentle sweetness that ignited a spark between them. But now, the dynamic had shifted; Katrina was taking the lead, her desires bubbling to the surface, passionate and fervent. Jarvis felt an electric thrill as he guided her, still blindfolded, out of the steamy bathroom. Water droplets cascading playfully to the floor, creating a soft patter that echoed in the dimly lit room. As he walked her to the foot of the bed, Katrina's senses now heightened; she could feel something beneath her feet, a sensation both foreign and delightful. It was soft and lush like stepping onto a fluffy carpet that seemed almost alive with movement. Jarvis had thoughtfully laid out delicate petals, in a whimsical path leading from the bathroom to their shared sanctuary in the bedroom.

They glimmered faintly in the ambient light, adding an enchanting touch to this intimate setting. The petals were scattered, not only along their path, but also artfully strewn across the bed covers, that still held traces of moisture from their earlier adventures. The setting was tantalising, and stirred something deep within them both. With deliberate care, Jarvis guided Katrina down onto this floral tapestry before him; he scooped her up gently into his arms, as if she were made of porcelain, then placed her softly onto the bed, a gesture filled with reverence for both her body and spirit. The atmosphere buzzed with unspoken anticipation as they prepared to explore this intoxicating connection further. Katrina was wild with desire, her every need ignited by an excitement, that was now surging through her like a lightning bolt, leaving her breathless and craving more. Jarvis showered her with kisses, that started delicately at her ankles. Each soft touch sent ripples of anticipation coursing through her body. By the time he finally reached her mouth, a fire had been ignited within Katrina; she could no longer contain herself. She eagerly reached for his manly parts, guiding him into her with a sense of urgency, that spoke volumes about their shared passion. Overcome with an electrifying joy, that coursed through their veins like molten lava, they both surrendered to the fervour of the moment. Their lovemaking became an exhilarating whirlwind, a wild and frenzied dance, where they thrashed about and rolled over one another in a tangle of limbs and laughter.

The space around them was transformed into a sensual paradise, as red petals rained down like confetti from some romantic celebration, clinging to their skin and amplifying the intoxicating atmosphere. In a daring twist that heightened the stakes even further, Jarvis removed the blindfold from Katrina's eyes. The world burst into vivid colours as she passionately gazed at him, the heat between them palpable as they navigated this steamy rollercoaster ride of emotions together. Each kiss felt charged with electricity; every touch ignited new sparks of passion, until they finally reached a climatic finale, then collapsed in a heap on the bed.

It was as if all energy had been drained from their bodies, leaving only blissful exhaustion in its wake. A shared silence, filled with lingering echoes of pleasure and intimacy, enveloping them like a warm embrace after their recent exhilarating encounter. They slept curled up on the floor, enveloped in a delicate blanket of petals, that had cascaded around them, like nature's softest quilt. The vibrant colours of the blossoms illuminated the dimly lit room, creating an enchanting atmosphere that felt almost otherworldly.

Each petal, plush and fragrant, cradled their bodies as they surrendered to slumber, lost in a dreamscape where time ceased to exist. The gentle fragrance of blooming flowers, mingled with the stillness of the night, wrapping them in a sensory embrace that soothed their souls. In this serene moment, they were not just resting; they were intertwined with the beauty and essence of life itself, captured in a perfect snapshot of tranquillity and peace.

Chapter Twenty-Eight
Surprise

As Lorraine lay nestled in Steve's warm and comforting arms, a sense of bliss enveloped her like a cosy blanket. She gazed up at the twinkling stars scattered across the night sky. Each star shimmered with possibilities, illuminating the thoughts, that were swirling in her mind. At that moment, she felt an undeniable certainty wash over her…it was time! Time to share what had been blossoming in her heart. Yet, despite this overwhelming feeling of rightness, she grappled with uncertainty about how to articulate those heartfelt emotions. The words danced just out of reach, teasing her with their elusiveness. But deep down, amid the gentle sounds of the night and the warmth radiating from Steve's embrace, Lorraine knew this was the moment to express what truly mattered most to her. It was now or never; beneath that vast canvas of stars, she felt an exhilarating mix of anticipation and joy bubbling within her.

"Steve."
"Yes."
"You know I love you, don't you?"
"You know I do, and you know I love you more."
"I have something I need to say, and I'm not sure how you will react."
"Oh?" Steve, now sitting up, felt dread begin running through his veins.

Lorraine gently took his hand and guided it to rest on her stomach, a gesture filled with warmth and anticipation. As he sat there, in the meadow surrounded by flowers, initially puzzled by her subtle cue, he took a moment to grasp the significance of the unfolding moment.

After a few heartbeats of contemplation, realisation dawned on him like the first rays of sunlight breaking through a cloudy sky. His eyes widened in astonishment, sparkling with joy and wonder as the incredible news sank in. A radiant smile blossomed on his face, illuminating the room with pure happiness, as if he had just uncovered a hidden treasure. The air around them shimmered with excitement, encapsulating their shared thrill in that magical moment of discovery.

"You're?"
"Yes."
"Oh my God! Oh my God! Oh wow!" Steve pulled her in, hugged and kissed Lorraine, then jumped up and screamed as loud as he could, "WOOOHOOOO!" Steve pulled Lorraine up, hugged and kissed her again, then rubbed her belly. "I'm going to be a dad! Oh my God, who else knows?"
"Just you, me, and Susan. She didn't say anything, just gave me the box, guided me to the toilet, and checked after."
"I'm so frigging happy. You make me so frigging happy. Wait, so the wine wasn't wine? I knew I had tasted it before."
"Yes, it wasn't wine. I'm so glad you're happy."
"No more heavy lifting, no more gruesome tasks. I can't have anything happen to you both."
"I won't take a back seat, but I have a deal: I'll still do all I can, and if I think it will be too physical, I'll let you do it for me."
"Deal. I'm going to be a dad."
"I will be a mom. That sounds so weird."
"So that's why you haven't been feeling well, and why you're so tired?"
"Yes, it's what first made Susan suspect I could be."
"You have to rest more, Lorraine."
"I will, now that I know I need to."
"I can't wait to tell everyone."
"Slow down, there's of plenty of time. I have arranged an appointment for tomorrow dinner, to see the doctor and get a scan."
"I will be there for everything. After the scan, can we tell Jarvis and Katrina?"

"Yes, and my mum."

Steve pulled Lorraine in hugging and kissing her, then he saw her shiver.

"OK, let's pack this up and get back into the house where it's warm."

Chapter Twenty-Nine
Maxine

Maxine was flustered, hot, and sweaty. She looked like she had just sprinted a marathon in a sauna. In fact, if there had been an Olympic event for sweating profusely, while trying to maintain some semblance of composure, she would have taken home the gold medal. As she paused for a moment to catch her breath, she wiped her forehead with the back of her hand, leaving a glistening trail, that could probably serve as a slip-and-slide for any unsuspecting bystander. It was one of those moments, where you wonder if the universe is conspiring against you, or if you simply forgot to check the weather before stepping outside. Maxine paused dramatically, hands on her knees, as she tried to catch her breath and regain some semblance of composure. Her heart was pounding so hard, it felt like as if it was auditioning for a role in a horror movie, thumping against her ribcage with all the subtlety of a marching band in full swing.

For a moment, she entertained the rather alarming thought that maybe…just maybe…she was experiencing some sort of heart crisis. After all, who wouldn't question their life choices when they felt like their chest was hosting an impromptu rave? With each beat echoing in her ears, she half-expected the paramedics to roll up at any second, complete with disco lights and a dramatic soundtrack. Ten minutes later, she had managed to pull herself together, her heart finally returning to a steady rhythm, thank goodness!

This was what packing for a holiday felt like, akin to wrestling a wild octopus while blindfolded. She couldn't help but chuckle at the absurdity of it all. Why did people willingly put themselves through this chaotic ritual so often? It was as if every time they planned a getaway, they signed up for an emotional rollercoaster, that made even the most adventurous theme park ride look like a leisurely stroll in the park.

Was it the allure of sandy beaches and exotic locales that drew them in, or were they secretly masochists who enjoyed the thrill of near-panic each time they misplaced their passport? The mind boggled! All Maxine was doing was packing her suitcases, but at this point, it felt less like a simple chore, and more like she was training for an Olympic sweating competition. Seriously, it looked like she had just stepped out of a sauna! The amount of perspiration that had accumulated on her body, would have filled a small kiddie pool. She might as well have been auditioning for the role of 'Sweaty Packing Pro', with the way her clothes now clung to her. Those wet patches were not only under her boobs, oh no! They were also proudly displayed on her love handles, making them glisten like they were winning some sort of bizarre beauty contest. And let's not even talk about the river of sweat trickling down her back; it was as if she had just finished running a marathon, while simultaneously trying to fold a fitted sheet.

At this rate, if anyone asked if she had packed extra clothes, they'd probably get an emphatic "do I look dry enough to you?" as a response! So back into the shower Maxine went. It was her second time that morning, and let me tell you, it was only two in the morning! I mean, at this rate, she might as well set up a little camp in there. Who needs a spa day when you can have a shower marathon, right in your own bathroom? Apparently, she had decided to embrace her inner mermaid, because between the first shower and this heroic second performance, she must have transformed into Aqua woman. I can just imagine her singing away to the shampoo bottles, like they're her backup singers while water cascades around her, like she's starring in an epic music video.

It's like she thought she'd missed the memo about needing to wash off all evidence of sleep, as if it were some sort of crime! Maxine's mind was like a chaotic carnival, with random thoughts and feelings bouncing around like hyperactive clowns on pogo sticks. It was, as if her brain had decided to host an impromptu party, and every idea and emotion was invited, whether they belonged there or not! One moment she'd be contemplating the meaning of life, while the next she'd remember that she left her laundry in the washing machine three days ago. With each passing second, her mental space resembled a jumbled mess of sticky notes on a refrigerator door, during a toddler's art project. Colourful, but utterly nonsensical!

And all this chaos was unfolding, because Maxine was gearing up for her very first holiday. Yes… her inaugural adventure out of the country, soaring through the skies on an actual plane! You know, the kind with wings and everything. As she packed her bags with excitement, that could rival a toddler at a candy store, a familiar foe began to creep in: anxiety. It was like that uninvited guest who shows up at a party and just won't leave. Suddenly, the thought of being thousands of feet above ground, in a giant metal tube, sent her stomach into acrobatics, that would make even the most seasoned gymnast green with envy.
How could something as thrilling as exploring new horizons, also feel like stepping onto an amusement park ride designed by a mad scientist? Maxine started to feel sick, her mind racing faster than the plane would ever go, thinking of every possible scenario, from missing her flight, to being trapped next to someone who smells like old cheese.

"Are you OK up there, Maxine?" asked Demetrio, snapping Maxine back to reality.
"Could you possibly help with my cases?" asked Maxine.

Demetrio sauntered upstairs, feeling like a hero ready to conquer whatever challenge lay ahead. With all the confidence of a toddler attempting to lift a car, he reached down to grab one of the cases. But instead of triumphantly hoisting it into the air, he quickly discovered that it didn't budge, not even an inch! The weight of that case held it firmly in place, as if it were a stubborn cat refusing to be moved from its sunny spot on the floor. It was as if the suitcase had declared, "Not today, my friend!" Demetrio stood there for a moment, contemplating whether he should negotiate with it, or just break out into interpretive dance to express his frustration.

They needed help, and the only one Maxine could think of was Lorraine. Demetrio decided they needed some muscle, so he called on McMatters.

"I'm sorry, Steve. I hope you weren't sleeping?"
"What's wrong, Demetrio?"
"We can't pick the cases up off the floor. I think I'm getting old."
"On my way, don't worry."

McMatters and Lorraine

As Steve and Lorraine pulled into the driveway of Lorraine's house, the clock announced that it was now two twenty in the morning. At this ungodly hour, time was not exactly what you'd call a generous friend to Maxine and Demetrio. In fact, it seemed to be playing a cruel joke, as they had only Forty minutes to reach the airport, a destination that was a daunting forty-five minutes away under ideal conditions, two frantic souls racing against the clock. Their hearts pounding like bass drums in a marching band, while their brains processed an escalating sense of panic, akin to trying to solve a Rubik's Cube during an earthquake.

Maxine glanced at Demetrio; his eyes wide with disbelief, as if someone had just suggested they swim across a shark-infested ocean instead of taking an Uber. With bags half-packed and caffeine levels at zero, their adventure quickly morphed into an impromptu episode of "Survivor: Airport Edition." Would they make it on time? Or would this be another tale added to their collection of travel disasters? The suspense was palpable!

"Have you booked something?" asked Lorraine.

"No," said Demetrio.

"I thought I'd drive and leave the car at the airport."

"You won't get there until next week, at the speed you drive Demetrio. Jump in, I will take you," said Steve.

Everyone piled into the car like sardines in a can, with Steve at the wheel, ready to break every speed limit known to humankind. With the road stretching out before them like an empty canvas, he decided that today was not a day for leisurely driving; oh no, today was about testing the limits of both his car and their collective sanity! He slammed his foot down on the accelerator, as if it had personally offended him. The speedometer spun faster than a rollercoaster ride at peak season, and they zoomed past landmarks that would make any local blink twice in disbelief. If luck was on their side, and with Steve driving, one could only hope their mad dash would get them to the airport, just in time for take-off.

"Are you going to?" Steve asked Lorraine quietly.

"Mum, I'm glad you're already sitting down and buckled up, because I need to say something."

"Are you waffling again, Lorraine? Spit it out."

"You're going to be a nana or grandma," blurted out Lorraine, like ripping off a bandage quickly.

"Oh, my word, you are? I am?"

"Yep, how do you feel?" Lorraine asked.

"Ummm, shocked."

"Congratulations, Lorraine and Steve. I'm so happy for you," said Demetrio.

"Thanks, Demetrio. I'm very happy indeed," replied Steve.

"Just promise me one thing Lorraine, that you will do a better job than I did," Maxine blubbered, tears rolling down her face.

They pulled up at the drop-off spot at the airport, and in a whirlwind of emotions, they quickly embraced like they were trying to squeeze out every ounce of affection.

"Have a nice holiday, Goodbye!" they embraced, as if saying farewell for several years, rather than just a short trip. Steve and Lorrain drove back and returned to the comfort of their home. Now it's time for some well-deserved sleep. They collapsed into bed, as if it's a fluffy cloud calling them home, ready to dream about all the adventures that lay ahead. If only their pillows didn't have such a knack for stealing dreams!

Chapter Thirty
The Office

Jarvis and Katrina were already at the office when McMatters and Lorraine finally arrived. Jarvis had an unmistakable grin plastered across his face, radiating so much joy and excitement, that it seemed to fill the room. Meanwhile, Katrina was not just happy; she appeared to be rejuvenated in a way that caught everyone's attention. The bruises that had once marred her complexion were now fading, skilfully concealed beneath a layer of makeup, that accentuated her features rather than hiding them. Most notably, she no longer moved with the same stiffness, that had characterised her movements before. Her posture was more relaxed, suggesting a newfound sense of comfort and ease. It was heartening to see her transformation; it felt like a breath of fresh air amidst the usual office hustle and bustle.

Jarvis couldn't help but chuckle as he observed McMatters bouncing around like a kid in a candy store, his enthusiasm palpable and infectious. The man's eyes sparkled with a sense of wonder and anticipation, that was hard to ignore. On the other hand, Lorraine sat nearby, her exhaustion evident in the way she slumped slightly in her chair. Her weary expression made Jarvis consider whether her fatigue stemmed from the pesky bug she had been battling recently; after all, it had knocked her out for a few days. Despite her obvious tiredness, there was also an unmistakable glimmer of excitement in her eyes, as she watched McMatters revelling in the moment. It was a curious contrast, two people experiencing such different states, yet somehow both caught up in the same thrilling atmosphere of anticipation and joy. McMatter's gaze shifted to Lorraine, who met his eyes with a brief but meaningful nod, signalling her approval of the course of action he was about to take. It was a subtle yet powerful exchange; in that moment, their unspoken understanding filled the air between them. McMatters felt a wave of reassurance wash over him, knowing that Lorraine stood firmly behind him. Her affirmation ignited a spark of determination within him as he prepared to move forward with confidence, ready to tackle whatever challenges lay ahead.

"Jarvis, I have some news. Demetrio and Maxine are on their way to Italy. We took them to the airport first thing this morning," said McMatters.

"That's good."

"Mum was scared; it would be her first time on a plane," said Lorraine.

"... and we are having a baby," added McMatters.

"Wait, what? You're pregnant?" asked Jarvis.

"I am," said Lorraine. Jarvis jumped up, shook McMatters' hand, hugged Lorraine, then kissed Katrina.

"We should celebrate," said Jarvis.

"There's something we need to deal with first, and we'll need Katrina's input on this," said Lorraine.

"My brother, well, so-called brother," said Katrina.

"How would you like it dealt with? It's only fair you get a say." asked Lorraine.

"Drop-kick his arse must be first, but it seems he doesn't learn. He just looks at everything and wants revenge, even if he caused the problem to begin with." said Katrina.

"I had noticed," said McMatters.

"His first mistake was the attack here. It wasn't needed. No one wanted it... many died."

"You know we didn't want that to happen," said Jarvis.

"Yes, it was all on him. Don't worry, everyone knows that now! His second mistake was not helping to find me. Third was not visiting, not calling...nothing. So now he needs a lesson, but he won't learn from it; he will just seek revenge," said Katrina.

"So, he's bubbling over at the minute, planning the next revenge?" asked Lorraine.

"If I were to bet on him doing just that, I'd win hands down." said Katrina.

McMatters casually poured himself and Jarvis a generous drink, the golden liquid swirling enticingly in their glasses. Meanwhile, Lorraine busied herself with the task of mixing a cocktail for Katrina, her movements fluid and practiced as she skilfully combined ingredients. The atmosphere was relaxed yet charged with anticipation, each clink of the glass echoing a sense of camaraderie among them. The drinks not only served to quench their thirst, but also acted as a social lubricant, setting the stage for conversations, that would soon flow just as freely as the drinks themselves.

"Lorraine, oh bless, that's your drink," said Katrina.
"And I can't drink" Lorraine pats her stomach, "do help yourself to it Katrina."
"Thank you."
"I think we should call in the Bennetts and Santos. While we wait for them to arrive, we will decide how to deal with Blythe," said Jarvis.

McMatters and picked up the phone and called both family leaders.
Jarvis felt an overwhelming sense of empathy for Katrina, acutely aware that she was grappling with a decision that weighed heavily on her heart and mind. The internal struggle of contemplating life or death, is not one to be taken lightly; it's a burden that can twist the very fabric of one's existence into knots of despair.
Jarvis understood that this wasn't merely about choosing to live or to die, it was about the profound emotional turmoil, the haunting questions, and the relentless what-ifs that danced around her thoughts, like shadows in the night. In moments like these, where hope seems dim and darkness looms large, Jarvis recognised just how tough it must be for her to navigate such a perilous crossroads. The weight of this decision could easily crush anyone under its pressure, and he

wished he could somehow lighten her load, or offer Katrina a glimmer of hope amidst the turmoil she faced.

Chapter Thirty-One
Detective Winters

Detective Winters had been grappling with the challenges of her new role ever since she took over from the esteemed Detective Jackson. Initially, she believed that her difficulties stemmed from the complexities of the job itself, an intricate tapestry of investigations, suspects, and evidence that required sharp intuition and keen analytical skills. However, as time went on, it became increasingly clear to Winters, that her struggle was not simply about the demands of being a detective. Rather, it was about stepping into the formidable shoes left behind by Detective Jackson. Jackson had been a revered figure in their precinct, renowned not only for his exceptional detective work, but also for his ability to inspire and lead his team with unwavering confidence, that was until he went off course.

As Winters tried to navigate her new responsibilities, she found herself constantly comparing her own leadership style to his. It felt as if she were merely a caretaker of a legacy, rather than an authority in her own right, a steward looking after her team rather than their true leader. This realisation weighed heavily on her heart. Each day brought forth fresh reminders of Jackson's influence: the way his former team members would speak of him, with both admiration and nostalgia, often referring to how he handled cases, or motivated them during tough times. In those moments, Winters could feel their eyes upon her, not with disdain or criticism, but rather with an expectation, that she could fill the void he had left behind. Determined not to let this sentiment deter her resolve, Detective Winters began redefining what it meant to lead this talented group. She focused on forging genuine connections with each member of the team, while respecting Jackson's legacy; doing so allowed her to carve out a place for herself within this already established dynamic. In embracing both the challenge and opportunity before her, she sought not just to uphold Jackson's standards, but also to bring forth her own unique perspective… one where collaboration and innovation thrived alongside tradition.

As Detective Winters continued this journey of growth and self-discovery within her role as leader, she realised that while standing in someone else's shoes can be daunting, it also provides invaluable lessons in resilience and adaptation, qualities essential for any successful detective navigating through life's complexities. So far, Detective Winters had not managed to secure anyone for any crime, which frustrated her to an almost unbearable degree. It wasn't merely the inability to press charges that gnawed at her; it was the disheartening reality that not a single shred of evidence could be uncovered in any of her investigations. The crime scenes she encountered were all too pristine, as if they had been meticulously scrubbed clean of any trace, that could lead to a suspect. There were no DNA samples left behind, no fingerprints lingering on surfaces, and distressingly few witnesses who might have seen or heard anything out of the ordinary. Each day felt like a relentless battle against the invisible forces obscuring the truth, pushing her further into a corner of frustration and determination.

The phone began to shrill insistently, cutting through the silence of the room like a persistent alarm. Part of her wanted to ignore the call, to allow it to ring unanswered, as she feared that it might be yet another case, another tangled mystery that she simply could not solve. The weight of past failures loomed over her, casting a shadow on her confidence and making her hesitate. However, despite this inner turmoil and doubt that gnawed at her resolve, she took a deep breath and answered anyway. The decision felt both daunting and inevitable; after all, every ringing phone held the potential for new challenges or unexpected breakthroughs in her line of work.

"Detective Winters here."

"I have a child with me who says he's found a body."

"Have you been to the location, PC?"

"I'm about to check the scene, but I've never done this before. Would you come to the site please, Detective?"

"What's your name, PC?"

"PC Taitington."

"Can you put the child in a room, call his parents, and get someone to stay with him? We need a statement. I will come now."

"Thank you, Detective Winters."

The Shopping Centre

PC Taitington and Detective Winters proceeded to the location provided by the child, only to quickly realise that their task would require considerable time and effort, due to the substantial size of the old shopping centre. This expansive structure, with its numerous corridors and a multitude of stores, presented a challenging environment for their search. The vast layout could easily lead them astray, complicating their mission to locate the specific area mentioned by the child. Given these circumstances, both officers understood, that patience and a meticulous approach would be essential in navigating this labyrinth space effectively.

"I hope you have no plans tonight, Taitington. This might take all day."

"It's the start of my shift."

"How long have you been a police officer, Taitington?"

"I passed my training one month ago and got assigned to the station."

Detective Winters now grasped the rationale behind the officer's request for a more seasoned individual to accompany her to the scene to confirm a body was in fact at the location. Given that she was relatively new to both the field of policing, having recently completed her training, and to this station, it is entirely understandable, that she would feel overwhelmed in such a critical situation. The prospect of encountering what could potentially be her first homicide victim would undoubtedly be a daunting experience for anyone in her position. A measure of support and guidance in navigating this challenging scenario is not only reasonable, but also essential for fostering confidence and competence in emerging law enforcement professionals.

"Okay, let's work floor by floor, shop by shop. That way, we can rule out and prevent any contamination at the same time. If we find a body, what do we do, PC?"
"We don't touch it. Wear gloves, call in the crime scene team, and limit all possible contamination."
"Okay, let's start."

Detective Winters was taken aback by the considerable amount of stock, that remained in several of the shops, which now stood vacant, shrouded in dust, and deteriorating with each passing day. The sight of these abandoned establishments, once bustling with activity, now echoed with silence and neglect. She found it particularly odd, that the thieves had not yet ransacked these stores entirely; it raised questions about their motives and methods. What could explain this oversight? Perhaps there was something about the remaining inventory, that dissuaded them? An unremarkable selection or items deemed too cumbersome to carry away perhaps?
Such anomalies only deepened the mystery surrounding the recent spate of thefts in the area, prompting her to contemplate what hidden factors were at play in this seemingly straightforward situation. Jackets remain suspended on their hangers, while shoes are carelessly strewn across the floor, positioned haphazardly as if the space were suddenly vacated in a moment of urgency. They then proceeded to the next shop, where they discovered that it had previously operated as a soap shop, specialising in an array of bath products. On the counter, they observed an assortment of

colourful bath bombs, each crafted to provide a luxurious bathing experience. Nearby, neatly arranged and meticulously stacked were various scrubs and sponges. Items essential for personal care, and located just two shops down from their current position. It was evident that there were numerous stores yet to explore, highlighting the vibrant commercial atmosphere of the ground floor in this bustling shopping area. Detective Winters, however, possessed a compelling community initiative that warranted her careful consideration. Before proceeding any further, she recognised the necessity of thoroughly contemplating the details of how this initiative would effectively function in practice. Additionally, it was imperative for her to communicate with Sergeant Cole regarding the proposal; his approval and authorisation would be essential before any steps could be taken to implement this idea. Thus, she understood that gaining permission from him was a critical component of advancing her plan.

Detective Winters was acutely aware that the process of locating a body within the confines of this area would likely span several weeks, if not longer. The challenges presented by the environment were numerous and complex, requiring not only her expertise, but also the assistance of additional personnel. Given the intricacies involved in such a search, such as potentially treacherous terrain, limited visibility, and the need for specialised equipment, she understood that collaboration with a team of skilled professionals would be essential to ensure a thorough and efficient investigation. To effectively manage and minimise operational expenses, Detective Winters initiates her strategy by directing her team to conduct a thorough search of the shopping centre.

This decisive action reflects a proactive approach, in which she seeks to maximise resources efficiency while ensuring, that all potential leads and evidence are meticulously examined in this critical location. By mobilising her team to the shopping centre, Detective Winters underscores the importance of immediate on-site investigation, as a means of gathering valuable information, that could aid in the resolution of the case at hand.

Chapter Thirty-One
Maxine

Maxine was consumed by worry as she sat in her seat on the plane, the cabin buzzing with anticipation and the low hum of engines preparing for take-off. She was buckled up tightly, each strap feeling like a vice against her body, a constant reminder of the journey that lay ahead. Her fingers dug into the armrest beside her with such intensity, that it felt as if she were trying to anchor herself to something solid amid her rising anxiety. On the other side, she clutched Demetrio's hand with an almost desperate grip, squeezing tightly as if he were her lifeline in this moment of turmoil. The warmth of his palm provided a flicker of comfort against the storm of nerves swirling inside her. As she fought to stay calm amidst the chaos of thoughts racing through her mind…thoughts filled with what-ifs and fears…. Maxine took deep breaths, reminding herself that soon they would be soaring through clouds, leaving all their worries behind.

The last of the passengers had finally boarded and taken their seats, yet a sense of unease washed over Maxine as the engines roared into life, their noise intensifying to a level that felt almost overwhelming. The vibrations coursed through her body, amplifying her anxiety as she sat in her cramped seat. She noticed that the doors were securely closed now, sealing them off from the world outside…. a barrier that felt more confining than protective.

In front of her, the air hostess was speaking animatedly, gesturing with her arms in what seemed like an attempt to convey important information about safety procedures or flight details. However, Maxine was trapped in a state of panic; every word and movement blurred together into an unintelligible haze. Her mind raced with worries and questions that swirled chaotically within her thoughts…what if something went wrong? What if they encountered turbulence? Meanwhile, she realised with mounting dread, that the stairs had been removed from the plane, leaving no possible escape route behind them. The finality of this action struck her hard; it solidified her feeling of entrapment within this metal tube hurtling through the sky. Each passing second intensified her worry as she struggled to focus on anything other than the rising tide of fear threatening to overwhelm her rational thoughts.

As the plane began to move backwards, a wave of anxiety washed over Maxine. Was this normal? Her heart raced with concern as she anxiously scanned the faces of her fellow passengers; some looked just as bewildered as she felt. The thought crept into her mind...is it safe for an aircraft to be reversing on the tarmac? Moments stretched into what felt like an eternity until, finally, the plane came to a halt. Maxine's mind was flooded with questions: What was wrong? Why were they moving in reverse when everything should have been straightforward? The uncertainty of the situation loomed large, amplifying her worry as she tried to grasp what might have gone awry during their pre-flight preparations. The plane began to turn, and with that movement, it surged forward. As it did, the vibrations intensified, a low rumble reverberating through the cabin, much like a warning bell. Each moment felt more pronounced as the aircraft accelerated quickly, gaining speed with an almost alarming swiftness.

Suddenly, there was that strange sensation...a fleeting moment of weightlessness as if gravity had temporarily released its grip on them. The metal tube glided gracefully into the sky, cutting through the air like a knife slicing through butter. Yet amidst this awe-inspiring ascent lingered an unsettling feeling in Maxine's stomach. She couldn't shake off the worry about what lay ahead in their journey through the vast expanse of unknown skies.
Maxine then noticed, with a mix of disbelief and excitement, that the air hostess had gotten up from her seat and started walking down the aisle of the airplane. Oh my God, she

thought, you can walk in the clouds! It felt surreal to her. Glancing upward at the overhead lights, she saw that the seat belt sign was still illuminated. As she sat there nervously fidgeting with her hands, anticipation bubbled within her; as soon as that sign goes off, she thought with a flutter of hope and exhilaration, I'm going to step into a world where it feels like I'm walking on clouds.

The air hostess moved gracefully through the narrow space between seats before returning with drinks for passengers, a small comfort amidst her growing anxiety. Moments later, breakfast was served; plates filled with fluffy scrambled eggs and golden-brown pastries were presented as if they were delicacies fit for royalty. She couldn't help but wonder: is this normal? Eating high above in what seemed like an ethereal realm among fluffy white clouds? The experience felt both wonderful and slightly unnerving. Would everything feel just as surreal once they landed back on solid ground?

Chapter Thirty-Two
The Office

Jarvis sat at his desk, leaning back in his chair as he watched everyone around him engage in light-hearted chatter. The atmosphere was lively, filled with laughter and the occasional burst of excitement. Amidst this buzz, his thoughts drifted to Lorraine. He couldn't help but wonder how she was doing and what her plans would be now that she was pregnant. Would she still be able to juggle her responsibilities at work? Jarvis had a nagging feeling that her role might change significantly; after all, being pregnant came with its own set of challenges and adjustments. He doubted she would be involved in any heavy lifting, or physically demanding tasks anymore. After all, taking care of herself and the baby took precedence over everything else. It made him curious about how the team would adapt to this new chapter in Lorraine's life and how they could support her during this exciting yet challenging time.

"Lorraine and Steve, how will things change around here now that you're expecting?" asked Jarvis.
"It won't change much. Yes, my body is going through some crazy stuff right now, but I won't alter anything yet. I might lighten the load though from time to time," said Lorraine.
"You won't be able to do the physical stuff, though, will you? I just wonder, with Blythe to deal with, will you be, okay?" asked Jarvis.
"I can still kick ass; I just might not be able to do it for as long," said Lorraine.
"I will help out when needed. Lorraine has said that she'll let me know if I need to take over, it will just mean I tag along where needed," said McMatters.
"I'll gladly help out. If Lorraine needs to kick ass and I'm around, I'll step in as much as needed," said Katrina.
"Would you, Katrina?" asked Jarvis.
"You bet your ass I will," said Katrina.

"Thank you, Katrina, that would be very helpful," said McMatters.

No one really had a clue about just how powerful Katrina could be, but everyone was buzzing with excitement at the thought of discovering her abilities. There was this electric energy in the air, a sense of adventure that made it clear that whatever unfolded next would be an experience to remember. The group laughed and exchanged playful banter as they speculated about what surprises might be in store. Would she summon a whirlwind of creativity or perhaps whip up some outrageous antics? Whatever it was, they all agreed on one thing: it was going to be a blast finding out!

Bennett strolled in alongside his second-in-command, and they looked like they'd just come back from a battle zone. Seriously, they were caked in blood and dirt, with mud splattered all over their clothes. Twigs were stuck in their hair and clinging to their jackets, making them look like they'd been rolling around in the wilderness for days. It was hard to believe that whatever they had just faced could leave them looking so rugged and worn out!

"What happened to you two?" Lorraine asked, her curiosity piqued by their dishevelled appearance.

"You know me," Bennett replied with a casual grin, "hands-on as always, not one to shy away from dealing out a bit of punishment here and there."

He shrugged nonchalantly, as if the idea of confronting challenges head-on was just another day in his life. It was a familiar dance for him, tackling problems directly and often with a playful attitude that masked the seriousness of the situation. The way he said it made it sound almost like a sport, where he revelled in the thrill of taking charge and setting things right.

Just then Santos arrived with his second in command.

"Wow, action in beds is better, Bennett" Santos remarked. they all laughed.
"Okay, guys, we brought you here because we all know we have a problem that needs sorting out," said Jarvis.
"My so-called brother." stated Katrina.

The room fell into a hush, not due to anything Katrina had said, but rather because everyone present felt the weight of the moment. They understood that it was about her family, her struggles and her journey. They instinctively knew how difficult this was for her. The silence wrapped around them like a thick blanket, filled with unspoken empathy and support, as they collectively braced themselves for what was to come. It was a shared understanding that echoed in the air, making it clear how much this meant to Katrina and why this conversation would be tough for her.

"Don't worry, guys, he has it coming. It's needed. There is one thing I do know, and that's how he thinks. This gives me an advantage," said Katrina.
"What are you thinking, Katrina?" asked Lorraine.
"First, I'll explain how he thinks and the actions he'll take. He lives for revenge. So, Jarvis and McMatters, remember the time he came to the club and lost his men? He'll want revenge. I'd check all cars and property, and Lorraine will need at least two more guards given her situation."
"Done," said McMatters.
"Next, Jarvis, he will try to come at you because you're with me now. He won't take that lightly," Katrina said, downing her drink. "Finally, Bennett and Santos, you were part of the team when he lost his men. Check your stuff and make sure it's all safe."
"On it," said Santos, nodding at his guy.
Bennett then turned to his guy. "I'll sort it, boss."
"I want to handle most of the punishment with my brother, but before I do, I heard he's scared of Lorraine. So maybe Lorraine has a chat with him first, then, I start the

punishment, and everyone else can finish. One thing though…I don't want him to be found… ever!"

Jarvis was completely taken aback by her directness, and surprisingly, he found that he liked it a lot. There was something refreshing about the way she spoke, no beating around the bush or sugar-coating things. It was as if she had this unique ability to cut through all the small talk and get straight to the heart of the matter, which made their conversation feel both invigorating and genuine. He appreciated her honesty; it made him feel like he could be open too, without worrying about pretence or what others might think.

Both Lorraine and now Katrina possessed this remarkable ability, each showcasing it in their own unique styles and approaches. It's fascinating to see how they both bring their flair to the table. Lorraine with her meticulous attention to detail. An ability to bring anyone down with just words. Then Katrina with her spontaneous creativity and flair. It's like watching two artists paint on the same canvas but using completely different palettes. Oh boy, thought McMatters this is going to be such a fun experience! I can't wait to see how they both tackle challenges in their distinct ways; the combination of their talents will surely lead to some entertaining and unexpected results!

"Katrina, welcome to the family," Lorraine said, passing Katrina a drink.

News

"Ummm, hold on just a moment before everyone rushes off! I have something truly exciting that I'd like to share with all of you!" Jarvis could barely contain his excitement.

"As you can see, our dear Katrina is here with us today, but not only will she be helping with the Blythe issue..."

McMatters glanced at Jarvis, curiosity sparkling in his eyes. He wondered if this was the moment Jarvis would finally unveil McMatters and Lorraine's big announcement, or if perhaps it was something entirely different and equally thrilling. The anticipation hung in the air, like a festive balloon ready to pop, inviting everyone to lean in closer and share in the joy of what was about to unfold!

"Katrina has agreed to marry me… yes… me! I can hardly believe it, but I am getting married!"

McMatters was absolutely gobsmacked for a moment; he stood there in stunned silence, eyes wide with disbelief. Then, after taking a moment to process the joyful news, McMatters looked over at Jarvis and walked right up to him. With a huge grin spreading across his face, he hugged Jarvis tightly before shaking his hand vigorously.
"Feck! That's fantastic news! I'm so incredibly happy for you both!" With excitement bubbling over, McMatters then turned towards Katrina and wrapped her in a warm embrace.
"That's right, you're stuck with us now, Katrina!" Lorraine chimed in with laughter, as she joined the celebration and pulled Katrina into another heartfelt hug. "Jarvis, congratulations! You truly deserve this happiness," she added sincerely.
"Damn. Excellent news!" Bennett shouted from across the room, with uncontainable enthusiasm. "Well done!" His voice echoed with joy and warmth that filled the air around them.
Just then, Santos made his way over to them with an earnest expression on his face. "I hope you both find nothing but happiness together," he said while shaking Jarvis's hand firmly.
The atmosphere was electric with excitement, as they all revelled in this wonderful moment of love and commitment. It felt like the start of something truly magical!

McMatter's gaze was fixed on Lorraine, his eyes glimmering with an inquisitive sparkle that seemed to dance with excitement, silently urging her to share the joyous news they both held. The atmosphere around them buzzed with anticipation, as if the world itself was holding its breath. With a warm and knowing smile, Lorraine nodded in response, her heart swelling with a mix of happiness and eagerness to unveil the delightful tidings they had been keeping close. Their shared moment felt electric, as if time had paused just for them amidst the bustling surroundings.

"Jarvis and Katrina already know this, but Lorraine is pregnant. I'm going to be a daddy."

"Oh my God, that's fantastic news!" said Santos. "Congratulations to you both and the bump."

"This won't alter any plans made," said Lorraine.

"I will take on more of Lorraine's tasks that are too physical, and Katrina will help out and shadow Lorraine," said McMatters.

"We have two special reasons to celebrate," said Bennett.

"We do, but first we need to deal with my brother," said Katrina, "then we party."

The room was alive with an infectious sense of happiness, radiating warmth and joy that enveloped everyone present. Laughter bubbled up from every corner as friends and family exchanged smiles, their faces glowing with delight. The atmosphere was filled with a palpable energy, as if the air itself sparkled with positivity and good cheer. Conversations flowed freely, punctuated by bursts of laughter, creating a symphony of goodwill that resonated throughout the space. It was clear that everyone had embraced the joyous spirit of the moment, making it an unforgettable occasion brimming with heartfelt connections and shared happiness.

Chapter Thirty-Three
Detective Winters

Detective Winters meticulously scoured the ground floor of the bustling shopping centre alongside PC Taitington. Their eyes sharp and alert for any clues that would unravel the mystery at hand. The air was thick with tension, an unspoken understanding that time was crucial in a case where every second counted. Just as they were about to conclude their initial sweep, the rest of Detective Winters' dedicated team arrived, bringing a highly trained cadaver dog whose keen sense of smell could detect even the faintest trace of human remains. This invaluable addition to their investigation offered renewed hope. After all, in cases like these, a single hint or whisper from the past could illuminate dark secrets and guide them towards answers that had long eluded justice.

"OK, guys, can we split up to cover this shopping centre a bit quicker? Can PC Jones, PC Maylan, and the dog take the top floor, while PC Barlow and PC Martins join PC Steele to cover the second floor? Then myself, PC Taitington, and PC Maitland will take the ground floor."

The team split up for a desperate search through the vast shopping centre, each silently hoping not to find any bodies. They needed open cases to tackle immediately, aiming for tangible progress rather than unresolved mysteries. As they navigated the labyrinth of shops and food courts, dread and determination coursed through them. The air was thick with tension, suffocating as shadows concealed secrets. Time ticked away relentlessly, pressing down like an invisible weight. Unresolved cases loomed over them, like a storm cloud ready to unleash its fury. With renewed purpose, they fanned out in different directions to unearth the truth. PC Taitington headed towards the electronics store, scanning for anything amiss among broken gadgets and screens. Meanwhile, PC Maitland cautiously explored what used to be a bustling food court now reduced to silence and desolation. Detective Winters began her search in an old music shop filled with neglected CDs and DVDs scattered like forgotten memories but found no signs of recent activity or struggle before moving on in hopes of better luck elsewhere.

Chapter Thirty-Four
Darkness Within

Blythe was completely off his face, having indulged in a
cocktail of substances, that he should have known better than
to mix. It wasn't as if he had never dabbled in drugs before;
on the contrary, he had flirted with various substances from
time to time. However, this occasion was different, as he had
chosen to combine an alarming mixture of crack cocaine,
alcohol, and cannabis, and then topped it all off with a dose of
LSD. This was not a great cocktail recipe to consume one
after another; it might have been manageable during the
chilled and relaxing moments at first, but soon enough the
tide shifted. What began as a mellow experience quickly
spiralled into tipsy episodes filled with unexpected joy and
exuberance.

These moments rapidly escalated into wild escapades, that
felt akin to buzzing bees darting around him, alive and
chaotic. It became abundantly clear that adding fuel to this
already volatile fire was an ill-advised decision. As the effects
intensified, Blythe found himself plagued by hallucinations;
strange visions crowded his mind, while bizarre objects
seemed to chase him relentlessly. Random things whizzed by
at alarming speeds a distorted reality that felt both thrilling
and terrifying. Shadows danced ominously around him,
haunting his every thought and movement.

At this point, he knew deep down that he had messed up, in
ways he could hardly comprehend. There was no turning back
now; he had no haven from this tormenting experience. His
thoughts were invaded by swirling shadows and indistinct
shapes, that merged into a nightmarish landscape of
confusion and fear. The once-familiar world around him
transformed into something unrecognisable, as Blythe
grappled with the consequences of his reckless choices, a
stark reminder of how easily one can lose control when
dancing on the precipice of substance abuse.

As Blythe began to emerge from the fog of the cocktail of drugs, that had clouded his mind, an overwhelming wave of hatred surged forth amidst the chaotic visions swirling around him. Slowly, as he settled into a semblance of clarity, more of the venomous thoughts that had festered within him started to surface. He found himself grappling with a newfound sense of control over the monstrous rage that lurked within his psyche. However, this control was tinged with peril; all he could focus on were those who had wronged him in some way, and a burning desire for vengeance consumed him. In this tumultuous state, Blythe felt emboldened by delusions of grandeur, he considered himself both King and God in his own twisted realm where he would orchestrate suffering for all who dared to cross him.

At the forefront of his vengeful thoughts was Jarvis, a name that ignited a firestorm of humiliation in Blythe's heart. Jarvis had made him look like an absolute fool during their last encounter, a scene orchestrated by McMatters, that only deepened Blythe's sense of disgrace. Then there was Lorraine, who had ruthlessly stripped away any remnants of dignity left in him; she took his vulnerability and treated him like nothing more than an errant child. To add insult to injury, there was also his sister, a betrayal so profound it cut deep into Blythe's core, who chose to align herself with what he perceived as the enemy, while belittling him at every opportunity. In this dark and festering landscape of resentment and fury, Blythe resolved that each one would pay dearly for their transgressions against him.

He envisioned retribution, not just as justice, but as an essential cleansing ritual, a way to reclaim not only his honour, but also his very identity from those who had sought to undermine it. The thought alone sent shivers down his spine; it was both intoxicating and dangerous, a potent mix that could lead either to liberation or ultimate destruction.

It was all Blythe had, to try and grasp in his induced state was how he would get revenge and when he'd do it.

Chapter Thirty-Five
Fly like a bird

Maxine was as giddy as a schoolgirl on the last day of term; she was about to take her very first flight, savouring her debut breakfast among the clouds, and enjoying every moment, until her bladder decided it wanted to join Cirque du Soleil. It had reached that critical point where it threatened to explode like a firework on New Year's Eve. So far, Maxine had heroically resisted the urge to unbuckle her seatbelt, hoping that if she stayed put long enough, perhaps nature would just give up and go away. She watched enviously as other passengers leapt from their seats like jack-in-the-boxes, striding confidently towards the loo without a care in the world. But now Maxine found herself in quite a pickle, with an internal monologue debating furiously against her overactive imagination about whether she could possibly hold out until landing, or if it was time for an emergency evacuation plan involving some rather creative aisle acrobatics. After all, she'd never walked in the clouds before!

"Demetrio, I need to go to the toilet."
"It's fine, don't worry, just go."
"What does it feel like?"
"To go to the toilet?"
"To walk on a plane."
"It's no different, Maxine. It's perfectly fine, give it a go and you will see."

Demetrio rose from his seat with all the grace of a giraffe on roller skates, allowing Maxine to wriggle her way through to the aisle. With an exaggerated shuffle that could have been mistaken for a peculiar dance move, Maxine edged towards the aisle. As she attempted to stand upright, a fleeting thought crossed her mind: "Ah, it feels a tad lighter on the feet today!" But alas, reality quickly set in as she realised it was merely an illusion, much like believing you can walk on air when you're just plodding along the ground.

Maxine made her way toward the toilet, her mind racing with thoughts about whether she'd fit into that notoriously skinny cubicle. It was about as wide as a pencil and seemed specifically designed for those who are more 'svelte' rather than 'flumpy' like herself. "If I were any fluffier," she mused internally with a chuckle, "I'd need a whole team of engineers just to get me out of there!" The prospect of navigating such tight quarters filled her with both amusement and trepidation, surely even Houdini would have struggled! But lo and behold, Maxine managed to squeeze in just in time! It was as if she had performed some sort of miraculous bladder ballet, gracefully pirouetting her way to freedom. Now that her bladder was finally empty, she felt an immense wave of relief wash over her, akin to a weight being lifted off her shoulders, or perhaps more accurately, off her bladder! It truly surprised her that she had managed to hold it for as long as she did; perhaps she'd unknowingly tapped into some hidden reservoir of willpower or simply channelled the spirit of a camel.

Today, however, Maxine felt like an absolute champion. She had not only survived the day's pressing challenges, but had also achieved what could only be described as strange yet remarkable feats, like facing down the ultimate test of endurance, that is public restroom availability. With each passing moment filled with triumphs both big and small, she was positively glowing with pride. Looking back at it all, Maxine couldn't help but feel a swell of gratitude towards Demetrio for insisting she come along; it turned out to be quite the adventure and let's be honest... who doesn't love an unexpected story about overcoming the odds involving bathrooms on a flight?

Chapter Thirty-Six
So Shiny

"Lorraine, since you know your jewellery, would you fancy coming up town with Katrina and me to the jewellery shop?" asked Jarvis.

"Oooh, I love all things shiny; count me in. Steve?"

"Maybe we could look at some things for the baby," said Steve.

"Oh, that would be nice," Lorraine said, getting excited.

"This will be so much fun," said Katrina.

"We will meet you both at the Jewellery shop, say around dinner tomorrow," said Jarvis.

"How about we have a meal while up there and make an afternoon of it?" suggested McMatters.

McMatter's heart raced with excitement as he pictured stepping into the baby store, it was a completely new world for him, one that he had never explored before, and each item seemed to radiate a magical allure that captivated his senses. He imagined which room in their house would become a cosy sanctuary for the baby, envisioning it transformed into a haven of warmth and comfort, filled with laughter and love. Would Lorraine have already considered these details? The thought made him curious; perhaps they should sit down together over dinner tonight, to discuss all these delightful possibilities. It struck him that this conversation could open avenues for shared dreams and plans, a beautiful step towards welcoming their little one into the world.

The evening ahead shimmered with potential as he anticipated diving into such an important topic with Lorraine, sharing hopes, ideas and perhaps even some apprehensions about parenthood. McMatter's heart raced with anticipation, as he realised that tomorrow morning held the promise of a momentous occasion: the scan of the baby. The mere thought sent a thrill through him, yet an undercurrent of uncertainty bubbled up within. He found himself pondering the mechanics behind this medical marvel; how exactly did they perform such a scan? And was it truly safe for both mother and child? Despite these swirling questions, an overwhelming sense of excitement took precedence in his mind. As he allowed his thoughts to drift like leaves in a gentle breeze, visions danced before him, images of tiny hands and feet, laughter echoing through their home. Would they be welcoming a boy or a girl? The prospect of having a son tugged at his heartstrings; after all, continuing the family name felt like an age-old tradition worth preserving.

Yet, he couldn't shake off the enchanting idea of having a daughter... a little girl who could illuminate their lives with her boundless curiosity and charm. This magical possibility filled him with wonder as he imagined her giggles ringing through their halls, casting joy, like sunlight streaming through windowpanes on a bright summer's day.

Jarvis felt an overwhelming sense of joy and anticipation at the thought of having everyone join them tomorrow, to help pick out the perfect ring for Katrina. It was a decision that filled him with excitement, as he wanted her to have nothing but the finest, after all, she truly deserved it. The prospect of selecting such a significant piece together was not just about the ring itself; it symbolised their deep connection and love. Furthermore, he cherished the idea of all of them spending time together, reinforcing the bonds that made them a family. Who better to share such a momentous occasion with, than those who mattered most? The concept of browsing through baby items also sparked a delightful thrill within him. Jarvis wanted to find something special for both Lorraine and her new little one to be, a gift that would convey his love and support during this incredible journey into parenthood. However, he found himself at a loss when it came to choosing the right present; perhaps wandering through the shops would ignite some inspiration, or spark new ideas as he explored the array of adorable baby products on display. The thought alone filled him with eagerness, envisioning the endless possibilities awaiting him in those bustling aisles full of tiny clothes and toys designed for little ones, a treasure trove waiting to be discovered!

Lorraine found herself consumed by a singular, overwhelming thought that dominated her mind at this very moment, and that was food, an insatiable desire for an abundance of it.

There was no specific craving gnawing at her; rather, it was the sheer notion of feasting on a vast array of delectable dishes, that captivated her imagination. She realised with growing urgency, that she had to pause her whirlwind of activity and indulge in a proper meal, yet the relentless busyness of her day had distracted her from this essential need. Now, as if a ravenous beast lurked within her, she felt an intense hunger, so ferocious that she could practically envision herself devouring something as absurd as a scabby pig! The idea struck her with both humour and horror, a vivid testament to just how starved she truly felt. Each passing moment only amplified the intensity of her craving, transforming what should have been mere sustenance, into an all-consuming obsession for nourishment. Lorraine couldn't ever remember feeling this hungry.

"Steve, I need food, like lots of food." Lorraine commented.

"Have you not eaten today?" Steve asked.

"Yes. Breakfast, two helpings an all, but I could eat a scabby pig right now, and I don't mean to share," said Lorraine.

McMatters got on the phone to the driver. "Can you do me a favour and nip out to get some food for us, please?" He asked.

"Sure, what would you like?" asked Lorraine's driver.

"Lorraine, what do you want?"

"McDonald's. Quick and easy: Bacon Double Cheeseburger, Large Fries, Popping Chicken Bites, a sugar Doughnut, and a McFlurry," said Lorraine.

"Damn, you are hungry. Jarvis? Katrina?"

"We're good, thanks."

He gave Lorraine's order and added his own, figuring he might as well. "I'll have the same, minus the popping chicken."
"Won't be long," replied the driver.

McMatter's then realised they must have some food readily available in the office! This decision came after Lorraine needed access to more food; with her pregnancy, her appetite had increased tenfold. McMatter's nipped down to see Paulie to arrange something
.

"Hi, Paulie," said McMatters.
"Hi, boss. Is all, okay?"
"Yes, it's great. I need a favour. With Lorraine being pregnant, she's feeling the need for food. Could we come up with some fresh fruit, etc., so if she's hungry and busy, she won't forget to eat?"
"No problem, leave it with me."
"Thanks, Paulie."
"Congratulations, it's a wonderful thing, you know."
"Thanks, I'm at a loss. I don't know what is needed. I don't know what Lorraine needs either."
"She will tell you as she goes."

Chapter Thirty-Seven
The Shopping centre

Detective Winters was utterly fed up with this wretched place. The oppressive atmosphere weighed heavily on her, and the dust was becoming unbearable. It was beginning to tickle her nose incessantly. A horrid smell hung in the air like a dark cloud, clinging to her senses, yet she couldn't quite identify its source amidst the choking haze of dust, that swirled around her. Yes, it was true, that she stood within the confines of an abandoned old shopping centre, a once-thriving hub of consumer activity, that had now fallen into disrepair and neglect.

Scattered across the dusty floor were remnants of a bygone era: items that had once been displayed for sale, now lay cracked and broken, lost relics of a vibrant past... now served as haunting reminders of what this place used to be. The layers of grime on every surface whispered tales of despair and abandonment, as she navigated through the desolate corridors, each step echoing in the stillness, like a warning bell urging her to hurry up before whatever lurked within these decaying walls could take notice. A crackle came through on the radio, almost deafening in the silent shopping centre.

"Detective Winters, come in," said PC Jones.
"Here."
"We have found an area where something has taken place. There are lots of footprints and scuff marks in the dust, but too much dust for us to get prints off."
"Whereabouts, are you? I will look on the map."
"Lot one hundred and nineteen."
"One minute, I will try and see where I am."
Detective Winters urgently located the faded shopping centre map, a relic of a time when bustling stores filled the once-vibrant shopping centre. As her keen eyes scanned the intricate layout, she identified the location marked as one

hundred and nineteen, which sparked a wave of memories. It was here that a grand three-storey department store once stood proudly. 'Debenhams' a name synonymous with quality and variety in retail. The sheer scale of the building had been impressive, its expansive floors teeming with an array of goods, from clothing to homeware. Now, however, it lay shrouded in silence and neglect, a haunting reminder of what had once been a thriving hub of community life and commerce. The stark contrast between its glorious past and its current desolation, sent an urgent chill down her spine; time was slipping away, and she knew that uncovering the secrets hidden within these abandoned walls could be crucial to solving her case.

"I'm on my way up," said Detective Winters.

Three flights of stairs, this was one thing she absolutely detested. Stairs had become a looming challenge in her daily life, and despite her efforts to stay fit, they now felt like an insurmountable obstacle. It wasn't that she hadn't maintained her fitness; rather, it was the relentless discomfort that accompanied each step, that filled her with dread. Lately, the tops of her legs would protest vehemently after climbing even a single flight, sending sharp jolts of pain coursing through her muscles. This agony didn't merely vanish; it lingered for hours afterward, as if mocking her attempts to stay active and healthy. The stairs were now not just a physical barrier, but a constant reminder of how much things had changed for her, igniting an urgent need to find solutions or alternatives, before they took over her life entirely.

"PC Taitington and Maitland, can you keep working on this floor and head to the ground level of the old Debenhams store?"
"Of course, no problem, boss," answered PC Maitland.

Chapter Thirty-Eight
Hunting

Jarvis and Katrina had been working diligently on a rather extensive list of potential hideouts where Blythe might be lurking, possibly sipping a fancy drink with an umbrella in it, while plotting his next grand attempt at revenge. This list wasn't exactly a short one; in fact, it was so long, that if you printed it out, you'd need a small team of Sherpa's just to carry the scroll! Given the sheer volume of locations on their hands, from suspiciously empty warehouses, to the odd treehouse that looked like it belonged to a particularly ambitious child, dividing the task among teams was truly their only option. After all, trying to tackle this alone would be like trying to eat an entire cake in one sitting, very messy and likely to end in tears and sickness. With teamwork as their secret weapon, they might just have a shot at catching Blythe before he could disappear! Bit by bit they called in different teams from all the families.

"Lorraine, you had the most recent dealings with Blythe. If you had to pick somewhere, where would you go?" asked Jarvis.
"I'd look at our most recent places first, as he knows we don't return for a long time, it's a safe place to hide out," answered Lorraine.
"Damn, they are not on the list. Well, they are now. Lorraine and Steve, can you and your security team hit them all?" asked Jarvis.
"So, let's see: steelworks, car graveyard, old mill, and book store? I'm not sure I can see him going to the docks or the mall, though...they're too fresh."
"I think I would agree," said McMatters.
"And you're okay to go, Lorraine?" asked Katrina.
"I'm not popping anytime soon," Lorraine laughed.

"Me and Katrina, with two guys, are going to his place, his garage, his treehouse. A grown adult with a treehouse…you couldn't make it up." Added Jarvis.

Jarvis phones Santos, to see if he can cover some other areas.

"Santos, how's tricks?" asked Jarvis.

"I'm doing well, thank you, Jarvis. How's your busy life these days?" Replied Santos.

"Well, that's why I'm phoning. Can you help in the hunt for Blythe and search some locations for me?"

"Sure. Where?"

"The jetty and Blythe's stash houses."

"Consider it done, speak later."

Next, Jarvis gets on to Bennett. "Bennett, how are you doing?"

"Not too bad. Busy, but in a good way. What can I do for you?" Asked Bennett.

"We are hunting for Blythe and need more hands."

"You say where, and we will look."

"The car showroom off the high street, the rowing club, the boarded-up station, and down by the canal. He has access to a narrowboat; it's jet black."

"I will let you know once they have been checked."

"We need him in one piece," added Jarvis.

"What are you trying to say?" Bennett laughs his head off.

With everything on the list ticked off, Jarvis is sitting there, pondering and hoping Blythe comes to his senses and they find him soon. After all, what Katrina blurted out about Blythe absolutely relishing his revenge, makes it sound like he's got a score to settle, that could fill an entire episode of a soap opera! It seems he has more grudges than a cat has lives, so many reasons to be vengeful, that one might mistake him for the villain in a particularly melodramatic play.

But amidst all this chaos, Jarvis can't help, but think of Blythe as nothing more than a wet lettuce, a limp, floppy excuse for a formidable foe! You know the type: all flustered and dramatic, but ultimately lacking any real bite. It's almost comical how seriously Blythe takes himself, while being so utterly soggy in spirit! Or other wise known as a wet lettuce, a soggy, floppy, ends in a sinky gooey mess that has no back bone or substance.

Chapter Thirty-Nine
Maxine

Maxine was bursting with pride, practically gleaming, she had done the unthinkable: she had left the country! Yes, folks, she has boarded a plane, an event that previously sat firmly in her "never-going to-happen" category, right next to winning the lottery and having Tea with the Queen. And let's not forget that moment of sheer wonder, when she walked amongst the clouds; well, technically it was just on her way to the loo, but who's counting? Imagine her delight as she munched on an airplane meal; while floating above fluffy white clouds, one could almost picture her in an ethereal dining room, set amidst cotton candy skies. But now, much to her chagrin and excitement alike, they were preparing for descent.

The thought of landing was another new experience on Maxine's ever-growing list of adventures, something so thrilling and outlandish, that she could hardly believe it was happening at all! After all this time pondering how it would feel like to soar through the sky like a bird, (or more accurately, like a slightly awkward chicken), here she was about to touch down on solid ground once more. What next? It was all a whirlwind of novelty for Maxine, and Demetrio found the whole situation utterly amusing. Watching her was like witnessing a child set loose in an enormous sweet shop, eyes wide with wonder and excitement. Each new smell wafting through the air seemed to send her senses into overdrive, while every touch felt as if she were discovering a hidden treasure. When she tasted something unfamiliar, her reaction was nothing short of dramatic; it was as if she had just unearthed the secret recipe for happiness itself! Demetrio couldn't help but chuckle at her sheer enthusiasm, one moment she'd be squealing with delight over the scent of fresh pastries, and the next she'd be dramatically swooning after sampling an exotic dish, that tingled on her taste buds like fireworks on New Year's Eve. It was a delightful spectacle, that turned even the most mundane moments into an adventure worthy of a sitcom!

The seatbelt sign flickered on with all the subtlety of a disco ball at a funeral, and suddenly Maxine was on a mission. She lunged for her seatbelt as if it were the last life raft on the Titanic, wrestling with it like it had just announced its intention to escape. Arms flailing and eyes wide as saucers, she looked like an octopus trying to juggle. Demetrio, witnessing this impromptu circus act unfold beside him, sprang into action to save her from imminent disaster, or at least from the embarrassment of being that person who couldn't secure their own safety belt.

"Hold your horses!" he exclaimed, half-laughing and half-concerned, as Maxine's panic threatened to spiral into full-blown hysteria.

It was abundantly clear that fastening a seatbelt had never seemed quite so perilous! As Maxine fumbled with the clasp, she glanced around nervously, half-expecting an overly enthusiastic flight attendant to pop up and yell, "Hold on tight, folks!" Maxine's mind raced as she contemplated what the landing would feel like? Would it be like the take-off, all quick and smooth, as if they were gliding on buttered air? Or would it be more reminiscent of her aunt Mildred's infamous pancake flip gone wrong, resulting in a chaotic crash landing that sent syrup flying everywhere? With each passing moment and the plane's ascent into the clouds, Maxine couldn't shake the image of herself soaring through the cabin if they hit turbulence. If only there were an instruction manual on how to survive this daring adventure, without turning into a human cannonball!

"Just relax, Maxine. It will be fine, you'll see," said Demetrio. Maxine was already gripping the armrest with such ferocity, that her nails were practically embedding themselves into the plastic, creating a rather impressive set of tiny divots. The irony of the situation was not lost on her; it was a classic case of premature panic. The plane hadn't even begun its descent yet, and here she was, bracing herself as if she were preparing for a rollercoaster ride at an amusement park. You could almost hear her inner monologue: "Why do I always forget to ask for extra gin during take off?" It seemed that every slight bump in altitude, felt like a daring plunge into the unknown, and Maxine's knuckles had turned whiter than her last attempt at baking!

Chapter Forty
The Shops

After an exhaustive search for Blythe at all the designated locations, which yielded no trace of him, Lorraine and McMatters exchanged glances of uncertainty, before deciding it would be best to postpone their search and venture into the shops instead. As they stepped into the vibrant, bustling aisles filled with an array of colourful baby items, a sense of overwhelming bewilderment washed over them both. Each shelf seemed to overflow with choices, adorable onesies in every imaginable colour and pattern, soft plush toys that looked almost lifelike, and countless accessories, that promised to make parenthood just a little easier.
As they browsed through this enchanting, yet daunting selection, they found themselves grappling with myriad questions: What on earth should they get? Would a new-born need tiny socks or oversized blankets? And what about sizes, was it better to opt for something slightly larger in anticipation of growth or stick with what was meant for infants? The unfamiliarity of it all left them feeling utterly out of their comfort zones. It felt as though they had been transported into a different world, one filled not only with adorable merchandise, but also with the weighty responsibility, that came along with preparing for new life. The experience was both exhilarating and intimidating, as each item seemed to whisper promises of joy and challenges yet to come.

"Let's see if Jarvis and Katrina are on their way; I'm starving," said Lorraine.
McMatters gets on the phone, "Jarvis, any luck?"
"Not yet."
"We didn't either, so we came to the shops. We'll look again in a bit. Do you want to join us?"
"On my way. I need to get Katrina the ring; I'm going to let her choose."

"Good plan, see you soon."

"Let's look in this shop Steve," said Lorraine.

"Lead the way" McMatters followed today; he wanted to get some things for the baby, but also wanted to sneak off. He had a plan, and Lorraine couldn't be there, he hoped Katrina could keep Lorraine busy.

Lorraine found herself wandering through the Cot section of the baby store, her heart racing with excitement as she stumbled upon an enchanting cot. Crafted from solid wood, this exquisite piece boasted a stunning white finish, that gleamed under the soft store lights. The intricate decorative spindles added a touch of elegance, making it not just functional, but also a beautiful addition to any nursery. Accompanying this remarkable cot was a plush mattress and an adorable mobile, that danced gently above, casting whimsical shadows, that would surely delight any little one. What set this cot apart from all the others in the cot section, was its ingenious built-in changing unit, complete with spacious drawers for storing all those essential baby items, like nappies, creams, and outfits, all neatly tucked away for easy access.

Lorraine couldn't help, but marvel at how thoughtfully designed it was; it seemed to encapsulate both style and practicality in perfect harmony. What truly astonished Lorraine was the price tag: only seventy-five pounds! It felt almost unreal for such an exquisite piece of furniture, that combined quality craftsmanship with multifunctional features. She stood there in disbelief, imagining how fortunate someone would be to bring such a treasure into their home, Lorraine just had to shout Steve over.

"Steve, we absolutely have to get this."

"Honey, if you love it, we're having it."

"Really?"

"Yes, really."

Steve had his hands full, with nappies piled up to his chin.

"I think we need a trolley," said Lorraine. A shop assistant noticed the pile of nappies and was already on her way over with a trolley.

"I think you might need this," suggested the assistant.

"Thank you very much. If we wanted some of the bigger furniture, could we get assistance?"

"If you note the code on the item and bring it to the till, we will have everything delivered, so you don't need to worry or carry anything around."

"Oh my God, that is wonderful. Thank you very much."

The assistant handed Lorraine an order slip along with a pencil, setting the stage for a delightful shopping adventure. With enthusiasm, they set about gathering essential items for the baby. Steve, his eyes lighting up with purpose, carefully selected three packs of new-born nappies and placed them into the trolley with an air of determination. Meanwhile, Lorraine busily added a changing mat, soothing cream, gentle wipes, talc, a magic potion for delicate skin and nappy bags, that promised to make light work of any smells. As they ventured further down the aisle, Steve spotted some charming drawers and a mini wardrobe that caught his eye.

With excitement bubbling within him, he began jotting down the codes for these delightful pieces of furniture. It was as if fate had intervened; not only were these items practical and functional, but they also perfectly matched the design of the cot they had chosen earlier! Their careful selection painted a picture of harmony in their baby's nursery, each piece harmonising beautifully to create an inviting space, filled with love and warmth. What an exhilarating experience it was to witness their dreams coming together so seamlessly!

"What now?" asked Steve.

"Do you have baby grows, vests, socks, and mitts yet?" asked Katrina.

"Oh my, no we don't."

"Katrina, could you help with all of that please? I need Jarvis for a second," asked McMatters.

"Sure."

So, Katrina and Lorraine set off to the clothing aisle while Jarvis and McMatters sneaked out of the shop.

Jarvis and McMatters

McMatters was thrilled, yet undeniably anxious as he finally managed to get Jarvis out of the baby shop. The impending excitement bubbled within him; he felt a mix of exhilaration and nerves coursing through his veins, making his heart race with anticipation. He needed Jarvis's assistance for something truly important, and in that moment, it felt like nothing less than a grand adventure was about to unfold. Traditionally, McMatters had always preferred to approach things in a conventional manner. He had envisioned asking Lorraine's father for his blessing, a time-honoured gesture rooted in respect and love, but that idea had swiftly gone out the window, as her dad she doesn't know, so despite this departure from tradition, one thing remained clear in his mind: he yearned to ask Lorraine to marry him.

However, there was one crucial element that needed to be addressed first, the perfect ring. As fate would have it, today seemed like the day for spontaneity; an impromptu decision began to take shape in his heart. With an undeniable desire burning bright within him, McMatters felt an irresistible urge to seize the moment and make this day unforgettable. The thought of presenting Lorraine with a beautiful ring and asking her to share a lifetime together filled him with joy and determination, he simply couldn't wait any longer! Jarvis was getting Katrina to pick her ring today after baby shopping, but before they had a meal, so it was a tight window to go and find one.

"Jarvis to the jewellery shop."

"Oh aye?"

"I'm going to ask Lorraine today at the meal."
"Oh, wow congratulations, that's fantastic! Yes! Let's go and get that ring!"
"Thanks' mate it means a lot."

They arrive at the shop, and as they step inside, they are immediately enveloped in a dazzling display of shiny diamonds, each one glimmering under the soft lights like stars in a night sky. He knows that diamonds are Lorraine's favourite thing; their brilliance and beauty have always captivated her heart. With this knowledge in mind, he decides that it must be a diamond for her this time. However, as he gazes around at the vast array of exquisite choices, each piece more stunning than the last, he finds himself momentarily overwhelmed by the sheer abundance of options.
There are so many to choose from: delicate solitaires, that sparkle daintily, intricate clusters that boast an explosion of light, and magnificent statement pieces that demand attention. McMatters made a splendid choice, by selecting a striking large, centred diamond that commands attention, flanked by two smaller diamonds one on either side. This exquisite arrangement totals an impressive two carats, creating a harmonious balance, that draws the eye to its brilliance and elegance. The entire composition is beautifully set in a luxurious twenty-four-carat gold band, which not only enhances the overall aesthetic, but also signifies the highest quality of craftsmanship and material. This thoughtful selection reflects an appreciation for both beauty and durability, ensuring that this piece will be cherished for generations to come.
With the ring tucked safely in his pocket, they are just about to leave the shop when McMatters suddenly remembers an important detail. He realises that they will be returning to this very store shortly, so that Katrina can select her own ring. The shop assistant, having already interacted with them during this visit, is likely to remember them, which could spoil the surprise he has meticulously planned. McMatters

feels a surge of determination; he wants to keep his thoughtful gift under wraps for as long as possible. This momentary lapse in judgement serves as a gentle reminder of the delicate balance between excitement and secrecy, that often accompanies such heartfelt gestures.

"Excuse me." said McMatters.
"Yes" the assistant utters, hopeful for another sale.
"Can I ask a favour?"
"Yes, of course."
"Soon we will be back here, so that his fiancée can pick her ring, and I don't want the surprise of my proposal to her friend to get out before I ask her."
"Mum's the word." said the assistant.
"Funny enough, she's pregnant."
"Well, congratulations on both occasions. Here, take this, and when you have the baby, come back. I will give you a discount on a baby bracelet." The assistant passes a card with a note on the back: thirty percent off baby bracelet, and signs it.
"Thank you very much" said McMatters.
"We best dash before they notice," urges Jarvis.

The Meal

Jarvis and McMatters sneak back into the baby store just in time.
"There you both are," said Lorraine.
"Have we bought the shop yet?" asked McMatters.
"Well, I did think about buying the shop. I mean, the baby business is always booming, but I figured I had enough to do at the moment."

Everyone erupted into fits of laughter, their joyous sounds ringing through the air like music. McMatters, caught up in the delightful moment, couldn't help but wonder if this amusing spectacle was something he could purchase. The idea fluttered through his mind like a playful butterfly, an enticing thought! Perhaps later, when the mood was right and the laughter had faded into warm memories, he'd enlist Jarvis to delve deeper into this whimsical possibility. What a delightful adventure that could be!

"OK, I need food," said Lorraine.
"Lead the way," said Jarvis.

The restaurant was just a short stroll away, making it perfectly accessible for Lorraine, who was feeling a delightful sense of anticipation. After considering her options, she decided on Chinese cuisine. which had been quite some time since she last indulged in its delicious offerings. The very thought of sweet and sour dishes, fragrant noodles, and crispy spring rolls was incredibly tempting; she felt as though the aromas were calling out to her, inviting her to savour the vibrant flavours, that she had been missing. With each step towards the restaurant, Lorraine's sense of excitement grew, envisioning a feast that would awaken her taste buds and bring joy to her evening. They arrived at the charming Chinese restaurant, that Lorraine had always adored, a vibrant establishment where the decor was a delightful dance of bold black and crimson hues, perfectly colour-coordinated throughout. As they stepped inside, the atmosphere buzzed with energy and excitement, setting the stage for a wonderful evening. They were seated at a prime spot on the top level, conveniently close to the enticing open buffet, that promised an array of delectable dishes. With her characteristic enthusiasm, Lorraine quickly dumped her belongings on the table, barely able to contain her eagerness. She promptly gave her drink order to the attentive waiter before dashing off with gleeful anticipation toward the tantalising spread of food that awaited her.

"Sorry about that, she's pregnant and starving." McMatters uttered to the waiter.

"No need to apologise Sir, it's nice to see. Congratulations."
"What other drinks could I get you?"
"Single malt, make it a double, a bottle of red, white, a pint of water, and let's see... diet coke."

They excitedly placed their belongings down and eagerly joined Lorraine at the sprawling buffet. She was truly in heaven, surrounded by an abundance of delightful choices, that seemed to stretch on forever. The vibrant array of dishes glistened invitingly under the warm lights, each one more tempting than the last. From sumptuous platters of roasted meats, to colourful salads bursting with fresh ingredients. Lorraine's eyes sparkled with joy as she surveyed the culinary marvels before her. It was a veritable feast for the senses, and her heart swelled with delight at the thought of sampling everything from tangy sauces to rich desserts.
They absolutely relished the vibrant atmosphere of the charming Chinese restaurant, where the ambient lighting cast a warm glow over everything. The delightful company of their friends added to the joy of the evening, as they gathered around a beautifully set table, filled with an array of delectable dishes. Each bite was a culinary adventure, bursting with flavours that danced on their palates. Laughter echoed through the air, as stories were shared and memories were created, accompanied by refreshing drinks that raised their spirits even higher. It was a wonderful blend of friendship, great food, and merriment, that made for an unforgettable dining experience.

Nearing the end of the delightful meal, with everyone feeling pleasantly stuffed to the bursting point, McMatters cast a glance at Jarvis and nodded. Now was the moment he had been waiting for, a moment brimming with excitement and hope. As his heart raced in his chest, he realised just how nervous he truly was; he had never felt anything quite like this before! The thought of embarking on such a life-changing journey filled him with both anticipation and joy.

He felt overwhelmingly lucky to have found someone as wonderful as Lorraine, who not only filled his life with laughter and warmth, but was also about to become the mother of their child. The sheer happiness bubbling within him made him feel like the happiest man alive; it was as if sunshine radiated from his very being. With that thought in mind, he stood up before everyone at the table, a gesture that drew curious glances towards him, and then knelt on one knee. In that moment of sheer exhilaration, he carefully pulled out a small velvet box from his pocket, its contents concealed but imbued with promise and love.

"Lorraine, I love you so much. You have made me the happiest man alive, and with that, I want to ask if you will be my wife. Will you marry me?"
The whole restaurant falls quiet; the only thing you can hear is her whisper, "Yes, I will marry you."
McMatters stands up, Lorraine stands, kisses him, turns, and the whole restaurant claps and cheers.
"Congratulations, you two! I'm so excited for you both," said Katrina.
"Congrats, mate," said Jarvis, shaking McMatters' hand.

Lorraine gazes at the exquisite ring adorning her finger, a radiant piece that sparkles with every movement. Its brilliance captivates her completely, filling her with indescribable joy. Each glimmer reflects not only light, but also the overwhelming happiness blossoming within her heart. In this moment, she feels as if she is floating on a cloud, on top of the world, basking in an enchanting glow of blissful contentment. She never imagined such profound happiness could envelop her; it feels like a dream come true, a beautiful testament to love and life's delightful surprises.

"OK, you two," said Lorraine, looking at Katrina and Jarvis, "we need to go get Katrina that ring."
"Ready when you are," said Jarvis.

"I will go and sort out the bill," said McMatters.

They walked slowly, almost as if in slow motion, their bellies full from a delightful feast. It seemed more like rolling than walking as they made their way to the charming jewellery shop. Despite their leisurely pace and slightly comical waddle, they eventually arrived at their destination. The excitement in the air was palpable, with the glimmer of jewels reflecting the sunlight and creating a magical atmosphere, that made their journey even more memorable.

"Katrina, any idea what type of ring you want?" asked Lorraine.
"I love emeralds, but it's traditional to have diamonds," said Katrina.
The assistant, her eyes twinkling with excitement, overheard the delightful conversation nearby. Inspired by the charm of the moment, she gracefully picked up a tray with an elegant design and carefully placed three exquisite rings on it. Each ring was a stunning masterpiece, featuring a dazzling array of sparkling diamonds interwoven with rich green emeralds, that seemed to dance in the light. The vibrant colours and intricate details of these rings created an enchanting display, that would captivate anyone who saw them, infusing the atmosphere with a sense of joy and wonder.
"Oh, my word, look at these," said Katrina after seeing the tray of selected rings.

McMatters and Lorraine stood back, snug in the latest chapter of their relationship. Katrina tried on each ring in turn, her heart fluttering with excitement as she admired the dazzling array of options before her. Each piece sparkled in the light, capturing her attention with a delightful display of colours and styles. As she slipped them onto her fingers, she relished the feel of the cool metal against her skin. She loved them all; they were like tiny pieces of art, but one cluster stood out prominently for her. It felt exquisite on her finger, a joyful embrace, that made her smile grow wider. The way it shimmered brought a sense of happiness, as if it was meant to be hers. In that moment, surrounded by shimmering jewels and the thrill of choice, Katrina felt a rush of joy and anticipation for what lay ahead.

"Is that the one that you want?" asked Jarvis.

It was a stunning one-carat emerald, vibrant and alive with a rich green hue, that sparkled like the lushest of forests. This captivating gem was elegantly encircled by a shimmering halo of diamonds, which collectively weighed another dazzling carat. The entire masterpiece was beautifully set on an exquisite 18-carat gold band, its warm, lustrous tones perfectly complementing the gemstones and adding an air of sophistication and luxury. This ring wasn't merely jewellery; it felt like a celebration of beauty and elegance, ready to be cherished for years to come!

"Yes, I love this and I don't want to ever take it off," Katrina said, then kissed Jarvis.

Chapter Forty-One
The Shopping centre

Detective Winters arrived on the 3rd floor, a wave of fatigue washing over her as she felt the persistent pains in her thighs. Each step felt like a reminder of the physical toll her demanding job often exacted. Her breathing was laboured, each inhalation a challenge as she fought to regain her composure in the dusty environment around her. It took her a full minute to steady herself, drawing in deep breaths and mentally preparing for what lay ahead before setting out to locate PC Jones, PC Maylan, and their loyal police dog. Detective Winters had indicated the signs to the old department store Debenhams.

"So, what do we have, Jones?"

Several markers were meticulously placed on the floor in areas deemed of particular interest within the crime scene, each one serving as a crucial signal to investigators. These markers could potentially indicate a wide array of evidence, ranging from latent fingerprints, that might reveal the identity of an intruder, to footprints that could trace the movements of individuals involved in the incident. Additionally, they may highlight scuffle marks, that could suggest that a struggle had taken place, or even denote actual physical objects, that warranted further examination. Each marker represents a piece of the puzzle, that investigators must carefully analyse to reconstruct the events leading up to and following the crime. The crime scene investigator then approaches these markers with a keen eye and methodical precision, thoroughly examining each one for any details or clues, that may shed some light on what had transpired in this place. This scrutiny not only aids in gathering evidence, but also plays a vital role in building an accurate narrative of the incident for any legal proceedings.

The first marker that caught their attention was the meticulous arrangement of chairs, they were not simply positioned in a haphazard manner, but rather laid out in a way that strongly suggested the presence of a recent gathering or event. This careful placement hinted at the interactions and discussions that had taken place, while also presenting an opportunity for forensic analysis, as each chair could potentially hold fingerprints. The second marker consisted of several distinct footprints imprinted on the floor, with each sole revealing its unique tread pattern. These footprints originated from different types of shoes, indicating a varied assembly of people who had traversed this space. Each footprint told a silent story about the individuals present, hinting at their identities or movements within the room. The third marker was particularly intriguing: what appeared to be drag marks leading from the cluster of chairs towards the elevator. These marks suggested some urgency or perhaps even distress, betraying a narrative of something significant having occurred just moments before. Next came the fourth marker, a simple bowl of water.... its presence both mundane and yet strangely out of place. It raised questions about its purpose: Was it left behind during an impromptu gathering? Or did it serve a more critical function in this unfolding mystery? Finally, there was blood...the fifth marker, that stood starkly against the backdrop of normalcy within the room. Its vivid crimson hue contrasted sharply with everything else present and served as an unmistakable indication, that something violent had transpired here. The presence of the multiple markers associated with each of the numbers scattered throughout this space, painted a vivid picture filled with layers of meaning and intrigue; together they created an atmosphere, thick with unsaid words and unasked questions, compelling one to delve deeper into understanding what exactly unfolded within these walls. If only walls could talk, she thought, observing the room. Something significant happened here, that's for sure.

Detective Winters gets on her phone, "Can we get the crime team down here to the 3rd floor of the Shopping, in the old Debenhams? The scene has been mapped."

Detective Winters surveyed the room with a keen eye, her instincts finely tuned to detect even the subtlest of disturbances. There was an elusive quality in the air, a nagging sensation that something was profoundly amiss, yet she couldn't quite articulate what it was. The shadows danced on the walls as if whispering secrets, and the faint smell of something burnt lingered in the corners. Each detail seemed to pulse with unspoken significance, the way a chair was askew or how certain items lay scattered across surfaces. Despite her analytical mind racing through possibilities and piecing together clues, this feeling eluded her grasp like smoke slipping through her fingers.

"PC Jones, could you take the dog down and check the same location on each floor?" asked Detective Winters. "Sure will, boss. Come on, Buster, let's go mooch," said PC Jones.

PC Jones caught up with his colleagues, PC Barlow, PC Martins, and PC Steele, on the second floor of the bustling department store. As they gathered near the entrance of the store.

"The boss wants us to look near the lift area for anything like what we saw upstairs."

"Was it bad?" asked PC Steele.

"It was more odd than bad. We know something happened there, but at this stage, it...some chairs, blood, a bowl of water, foot prints and scuff mark or movement mark."

As they approached the lift, the pristine condition of its surface was striking, akin to a canvas untouched by the hands of time. It appeared as if the dust had been banished entirely, leaving behind an immaculate sheen that reflected the surrounding lights. Not a single mark or fingerprint marred its flawless exterior, which seemed almost surreal in a world where wear and tear are commonplace. This level of cleanliness evoked a sense of calm and order, inviting them to step inside without hesitation or reservations about their surroundings.

"All clear here, boss. Even the dog has no interest," said PC Jones.
"OK, head down to ground level with the others and look at the same area."
So, all the police officers head down to the ground floor.

Chapter Forty-Two
Brace for Impact

Maxine was bracing herself for landing, her seatbelt firmly fastened across her lap, while her nails dug anxiously into the armrest of the seat, leaving faint impressions in the fabric. The aircraft was starting its descent when an unexpected noise…a disconcerting click followed by a jarring bang…pierced through the cabin's usual hum of engines and chatter.
Startled, Maxine instinctively turned to look at Demetrio, her eyes wide with apprehension.
It was as if he could read her thoughts that screamed, "Oh shit, what was that?" To soothe her rising panic and reassure her amidst the growing uncertainty in the air around them, he reached out and gently grasped her hand. His warm touch offered a momentary anchor against the backdrop of turbulence, that seemed to surround them both…an unspoken promise that they would navigate this unsettling experience together.

"Don't worry, that's the landing gear being deployed," said Demetrio.
Maxine could feel the engines rumbling beneath her, and their noise had intensified, vibrating through the cabin with an unsettling presence. The sounds were no longer a mere background hum. They had transformed into a cacophony that echoed her growing unease. Suddenly, without warning, the plane dropped in height, plunging downwards in a manner that sent a jolt of fear racing through her body.
The abrupt descent made Maxine's stomach lurch violently, triggering an unsettling sensation reminiscent of the exhilarating yet terrifying moments spent on a rollercoaster ride. It was as if she had been thrust into an unexpected freefall. With each passing second, anxiety clawed at her chest, leaving her to wonder what could possibly be happening to cause such turbulence in the air. Maxine could

now feel the plane's gradual descent; the drop was gentle, yet it seemed to amplify her growing sense of unease. Each moment brought her closer to the ground, but rather than instilling comfort, it only heightened her anxiety.

The air hostess was making her way up the cabin, a smile plastered on her face as she opened all the windows, allowing light to flood in. Why on earth would they do that? The very idea felt utterly absurd to Maxine. Why would anyone want to gaze out at what might be an impending doom? The thought of staring down at the vast expanse of land far below seemed more like a cruel joke than a comforting gesture. All she could imagine were those terrifying images of plummeting planes or turbulent skies; in moments like this, ignorance often felt blissful.

As she glanced nervously at her fellow passengers... some appearing calm and collected while others mirrored her anxiety. She couldn't shake off the feeling that exposing them to the outside world in such a precarious situation was nothing short of reckless. What if disaster lay just beyond those windows?

"Don't worry, Maxine, it's okay," said Demetrio, as he peeled each finger off to relieve the pressure of her tight grip.

"Can you open the window shutter, please?" Asked the air hostess.

"It's too scary to look."

"We are almost ready to land; all shutters have to be up I'm afraid."

Maxine lifted the shutter with a sense of trepidation and was taken aback by the perspective that greeted her.

The buildings below appeared tiny, mere toys scattered across the landscape, while the cars looked like ants scurrying about, oblivious to the vastness above them. As she gazed out of the window, she noticed how the plane was gradually reducing its height, an action that seemed to pull her focus away from her swirling worries. In fact, this descent provided an unexpected reprieve from the unsettling knots in her stomach. What had

144

once felt like a tumultuous whirlpool of anxiety now began to settle into a more manageable calmness, as if the very act of descending brought with it a soothing reassurance that everything would soon be alright.

Maxine wasn't expecting that looking out of the planes window would in fact help her to be calm and have a better sense of control. The air hostess returned to her designated area, her movements betraying a sense of urgency as she quickly dialled someone on the phone before taking a seat and fastening her belt.

Her heart raced as she observed the surroundings. The buildings had transformed dramatically, now looming much larger than before, their imposing structures casting long shadows over the tarmac. The cars below, which had previously appeared as mere toy vehicles, now resembled full-sized automobiles once more, bustling about in a frenetic dance typical of an airport environment. There were numerous planes gathered near the buildings of the airport, each one distinct and grand, their metallic bodies glinting under the bright sunlight. The runway stretched out before her like a vast canvas painted with different coloured lines that marked various pathways for take-offs and landings. This vibrant palette added an element of chaos to what should have been orderly operations, but instead filled her with unease; it seemed every detail was amplified and exaggerated in her heightened state of awareness.

Everything felt overwhelming yet strangely fascinating as she grappled with the enormity of her surroundings while trying to make sense of it all amidst her growing apprehension. The plane felt as if it had just hit the emergency stop button, abruptly jolting and shaking violently in the air. The flaps on the wings adjusted, working diligently to slow it down as they cut through the turbulent atmosphere.

Maxine once again squeezed the life out of Demetrio's hand, her grip a desperate plea for reassurance amidst the chaos. With a sudden jolt followed by a smaller bump, she could feel the ground rumble beneath them, an unsettling reminder of their precarious descent. The brakes screeched in a frantic attempt to bring the massive aircraft to a halt, filling her with an overwhelming sense of anxiety as she braced for impact. As they finally touched down, there was an unexpected eruption of applause and cheers from everyone on board, which momentarily broke through her worries.

Maxine heard someone in the background shout enthusiastically, "Fantastic landing!" Their enthusiastic clapping echoed around her like thunderous applause at a performance well executed, yet she remained unable to fully share in their joy. While relief washed over others around her, she still felt an undercurrent of trepidation coursing through her veins…a nagging fear that lingered long after they had landed safely on solid ground, she prayed she would get to see her grandchild.

Chapter Forty-Three
The Hunt Continues

Jarvis, Katrina, Lorraine, and McMatters looked at each other with a mixture of determination and mischief as they decided to continue the relentless hunt for the elusive Blythe. After all, how hard could it be to find one man in a world full of distractions like cat videos and lunchtime gossip? Since fate had conspired to gather this ragtag team of amateur sleuths together, they thought it only logical...if logic could ever be applied here to visit the locations listed on both their treasure maps. With an air of hopeful optimism and perhaps a hint of naiveté, they plotted their course with the enthusiasm, maybe they will get lucky.

They began their little adventure by visiting each location of the seven areas in proximity, like a group of curious treasure hunters on a rather unconventional quest. Since one of these locations is conveniently situated just a stone's throw away from where they currently stand, they decide to stroll over to the old bookstore, hoping to uncover any signs of life or perhaps even some hidden treasure...like that elusive first edition copy of "Wuthering Heights", that every bookworm dreams about.

Upon arrival, not wanting to be deterred by such trivialities, they opt for a more adventurous route and wander around to the back entrance, which is surprisingly unlocked. This could mean several things: Slater and his merry band of misfits were holed up here for ages, trying to hide from impending doom. As they step inside what used to be a charming little bookshop, they're greeted by a scene that would make any bibliophile weep...a graveyard of empty shelves and abandoned literary dreams. Scattered around are remnants of what was clearly not just an ordinary literary retreat: pizza boxes piled high like an unsightly monument to late-night brainstorming sessions of how to escape, cigarette butts littered about and smashed cans of pop making it look more like a student flat than an establishment dedicated to literature. Eerily silent yet oddly nostalgic, it feels as though all those beloved books have been whisked away by some mischievous spirit.

Despite their thorough search through this deserted realm of words and ink stains, nothing indicates that Blythe had ever set foot in this haunted haven.

They exit the bookshop's sorrowful remains and make their way towards Blythe's garage, the next item on their list. They arrive at the garage, and with no one in sight, Katrina opens it. They don't find Blythe, but instead discover old furniture that really needs to go in a skip, a lot of dust and old blankets. So, next they try Blythe's house.

"Let's go directly to the back door," said Katrina.
"You know him best," agreed Jarvis.
They open the gate to the garden and see the treehouse in the far corner.
"Me and Lorraine will check the tree house while we are here" said McMatters.

Jarvis gives a quick nod of acknowledgment as he and Katrina slip through the back door. As soon as they step inside, an overwhelming smell smacks him right in the face like a disgruntled cat on a bad day. It's an aroma so potent, that he instinctively takes a step back, almost stumbling over his own feet in disbelief. With wide eyes, he glances at Katrina, only to find she's sporting the exact same expression of shock and horror. Clearly, they're both questioning their life choices at this very moment. With their noses covered they bravely re-enter Blythe's house, steeling themselves for whatever olfactory assault awaits them next.

They begin their mission: moving stealthily from room to room, like two detectives in a particularly sticky mystery novel, determined to locate Blythe without inadvertently touching anything that might be deemed hazardous or

questionably sticky. Each room is approached with caution; it's less about finding the hostess, but more about surviving the scent-sational adventure that is Blythe's home!
McMatters lent a helping hand as Lorraine embarked on her ambitious quest to conquer the treehouse. As he finally reached the top, he was taken aback; it was unexpectedly sturdy and impressively well-constructed.

"Goodness gracious!" he exclaimed, "There's no way Blythe could have built this masterpiece; it practically had 'builder of the year' stamped all over it!" McMatters couldn't help but chuckle at the thought, that if only he'd put his DIY skills to work in his own garden, maybe he could have fashioned something just as remarkable for little Lorraine's impending arrival.

With a sigh and a shake of their heads, they decided it was time to descend from their lofty perch and reunite with Jarvis and Katrina in the house search.
"I need to warn you about the last time I was here," said Lorraine.
"Oh, why?" asked McMatters.
"The smell will knock you sick."

The Santos

Santos had already meticulously checked the areas on the list. Not just once, but twice, ensuring that no detail was overlooked. During his first sweep, he stumbled upon a homeless man huddled at the entrance to the jetty. The sight tugged at Santos' heartstrings; with autumn now firmly established, the air had turned crisp and decidedly chilly. Each gust of wind felt like icy fingers probing through layers of clothing, and he knew all too well, that spending too long in such conditions could lead to a bone-deep chill, that would take hours to shake off.

Determined to make a difference in this man's life, Santos rallied his men and instructed them to gather some warm items to offer relief: a few thick blankets to wrap around him for warmth, a large hot drink, that would provide comfort from the inside out, and two hearty sandwiches, that might stave off hunger for at least a short while longer.

Additionally, Santos reached into his pocket and handed over thirty pounds in cash, a sum that may have seemed trivial to him, but represented an invaluable lifeline for the man who was struggling on the streets. As he watched the surprise flicker across the man's face upon receiving both food and money, Santos sincerely hoped it would help him navigate through these cold months ahead. Santos told him about the disused mill as it might help keep the rain off him and help with the warmth.

Santos scoured the remainder of the jetty area, his eyes peeled for any sign of Blythe or his crew. After a thorough search, he made his way to the next location: the stash houses that Santo's men had been keeping under surveillance. When he reached the first stash house, he approached the door with caution. To his surprise, it swung open effortlessly, as if inviting him inside. His men quickly fanned out in different directions, each keenly searching for any trace of Blythe or his associates. However, upon stepping inside the house, Santos was struck by an unsettling realisation…the place felt unusually barren and devoid of life.

For a stash house typically teeming with supplies and perhaps even some loyal guards on watch, this was decidedly peculiar. There were no boxes stacked high with contraband goods or any signs of recent activity; it seemed as though they had stumbled into a ghost town, rather than a hub for illicit trade. The emptiness hung heavily in the air, raising alarm bells in Santos' mind about what might have transpired here and where Blythe could possibly be hiding now.

They moved three doors down to the second stash house and tried the door handle; it was locked, so they went around to the back. At the back door, they tried the handle, and it was open. Santos preferred trying handles before kicking in doors, as it was quieter. They entered, and his men fanned out again. All the rooms were bare…no furniture, no drugs, no weapons, no men, no evidence of life. It was completely empty. Santos got on the phone.

"Hi Jarvis, it's Santos. It's all clear, no sign of life. I'll get my men to keep an eye out, though, just in case," added Santos. "Thanks, Santos. Good work," replied Jarvis.

The Bennetts

Bennett stood in the middle of the car showroom, a peculiar sight, that left him feeling unsettled. It was strange and disconcerting not to see any cars in what had once been a bustling hub of activity. The only signs that indicated it had ever been a functioning business, were the tangled wires snaking across the floor and the empty desks, which seemed almost ghostly in their abandonment. Everything else had been removed, leaving behind an eerie emptiness, that filled the expansive space. As he glanced around, Bennett noticed the kitchen area. This would have served as a staffroom and showed evidence of some past activity.
However, it was clear that nothing had transpired there for quite some time. The fridge stood ajar; its contents long forgotten; inside were mouldy products that had decayed beyond recognition. Once identifiable items had transformed into unrecognisable masses of mould, resembling grotesque sculptures rather than food items.
This decay not only highlighted neglect, but also served as a cautionary reminder of how quickly spaces can be

transformed from vibrant workplaces into mere shadows of their former selves when left unattended.

Bennett and his team made their way to the train station, a location that had been shuttered for over a decade. This once-bustling hub of activity had fallen silent since a new, modern station, with state-of-the-art features had been constructed only few miles away.

As they approached the derelict building, it became evident that the station had been abandoned for quite some time, leaving behind an eerie atmosphere that hinted at its former glory. Crumbling walls and overgrown weeds encroached upon the platforms, serving as reminders of a vibrant past now long forgotten. This visit was not merely an exploration; it carried with it an air of caution. The dilapidated infrastructure posed potential hazards, and the team needed to be vigilant amidst the remnants of what used to be a lively transit point for countless passengers.

"Tread lightly here guys, it's an old building that's been left to rot" said Bennett, warning his men.

His team commenced a thorough search of the waiting rooms, the office area, the control room, and the ticket office, leaving no stone unturned in their quest. Meanwhile, Bennett meandered through the exquisite potential nooks and crannies, those charming yet concealed spaces, where Blythe could be hiding. The beauty of these areas was almost deceptive; their alluring aesthetics contrasted sharply with the seriousness of their endeavour. Every shadowy corner and every quaint alcove held an air of mystery, but it was essential to remain vigilant.

With each passing moment, the risk that Blythe could slip away undetected heightened significantly. It was imperative, that they approach this search with both diligence and caution, as overlooking even a small detail could have dire consequences in such a critical situation.

His men all returned, but it appeared that some commotion had taken place in the waiting room.

However, it was not believed to be linked to Blythe; rather, it resembled the sort of spirited antics one would expect from a group of teenagers seeking refuge from the cold. They seemed to have turned the space into a makeshift haven, where they could gather and keep warm, a safe place for them to hang out and share stories or laughter amidst their youthful exuberance. Bennett and his team next head over to the rowing club, which is on way to the narrow boat.

Chapter Forty-Four
Blythe's house

The further Jarvis and Katrina ventured into the depths of the house, the more the air thickened with a pungent aroma, that could only be described as a cross between old gym socks and something one might find lurking at the bottom of a very neglected litter box. With each cautious step, they bravely soldiered on, but not without frequent pauses to compose themselves. So far, they had avoided succumbing to the overwhelming urge to hurl their lunch and possibly breakfast … right there on the floor. It was a smell so persistent that it clung to the back of their throats, like an unwelcome guest who had overstayed their welcome, at a party where nobody wanted them in attendance. In fact, it was as if someone had taken all the undesirable odours, and decided to throw them into a food blender for good measure; they couldn't decide whether they were stepping deeper into an abandoned home, or a house of the dead!

As they meandered through the various rooms, a rather alarming trend emerged like an unwanted guest at a tea party. Dirt, dust, mould, and what one might delicately refer to as "evidence of a party gone awry," complete with an assortment of needles strewn across the floor, like confetti at a particularly wild celebration. Katrina's heart raced as she surveyed the chaotic scene, her mind whirling with questions. Was this disarray simply the result of some rather unfortunate house guests dossing about on their last bender? Or was it possible…. dare she even think it, but had Blythe ventured down that dark alleyway into the world of drugs? The idea sent shivers down her spine; after all, no one wants to discover their brother is going down that path. Is that why he's been so erratic and twisted?

Jarvis could hear the unmistakable sounds of McMatters and Lorraine trailing behind them, a symphony of coughing and gagging, that could rival any horror film soundtrack. It was as if they were auditioning for a role in "The Coughing Dead."

Lorraine, poor thing, was heaving like she'd just run a marathon, after inhaling an entire jar of pickled onions. He could almost picture her at the finish line, gasping for air while clutching her stomach in despair. Meanwhile, Jarvis pressed on with determination, reaching the last room in the house. With an exaggerated push he opened the door slowly, half-expecting to find either treasure or some terrible horror, that would send his companions into more fits of theatrical retching. What awaited him beyond that threshold?

When Jarvis finally mustered the courage to open the last door in Blythe's house, he was utterly unprepared for the shocking scene that greeted his eyes. While he had always known, that Blythe was scruffy and somewhat unkempt, he never could have imagined, that his living conditions would be so bleak and disheartening. The room before him was nothing more than a bare, lifeless space, dominated by a single bed, devoid of any semblance of comfort or warmth. There were no blankets to ward off the chill of the night, no clothes or shoes strewn about…just a grimy mattress, that spoke volumes about neglect and despair. As he glanced down at the mattress, Jarvis couldn't help but recoil at its ghastly appearance; it was covered in unsightly stains, each one telling an unspoken story of past mishaps, or perhaps even worse.
The thought of delving into what those stains might represent, filled him with an overwhelming sense of dread…he had no intention of uncovering any further horrors, that may be hidden within this forsaken room. Surrounding him was a complete absence of decoration; there were no cheerful accents, or colourful touches to lift one's spirits. Instead, what met his gaze were walls marred by graffiti. A chaotic splash of colours and words, that only served to amplify the room's desolation and neglect. This disturbing revelation left Jarvis feeling profoundly worried for Blythe's well-being; it raised numerous questions in his mind about how someone could endure such squalor. Had it always been this way?

Although the room had a rancid odour permeating the very atmosphere, it became apparent, that it wasn't the actual source of this lingering stench.

Jarvis found himself increasingly puzzled and anxious by this unsettling revelation, as they had meticulously checked every room in the house, leaving no corner unexplored. The oppressive odour seemed to weave its way through the walls, sneaking into their nostrils like a ghostly presence that refused to be identified. Each time Jarvis inhaled deeply, he felt an uncomfortable knot tightening in his stomach; how could such an overpowering smell escape detection? With each passing moment, his unease grew. What if there was something hidden away in the depths of this seemingly ordinary house? The fear of uncovering something far more sinister than mere rubbish loomed over him like a dark cloud. Where else was there to check?

"What about the attic? There's nowhere else left; it must be the source of that smell," said McMatters.

"I agree, can you give me a lift up please?" asked Jarvis.

McMatters stood with his feet firmly planted beneath the attic hatch, his posture unwavering despite the weight of the situation. The dim light filtering through the narrow openings cast eerie shadows, amplifying the tension in the air. Katrina, her brow furrowed with concern, helped Jarvis maintain his balance, as McMatters hoisted him onto his broad shoulders. With a mix of determination and trepidation, Jarvis extended his arms towards the attic hatch, grappling with its heavy frame. He lifted it gingerly, pushing it backwards with all his might. Each movement felt fraught with uncertainty, as he wondered what secrets lay beyond that threshold and whether they were truly prepared for whatever awaited them in that darkened space above. They all instantly gagged at the sudden smell, as a large waft drifted out of the attic hatch.

156

"I think we've found the source of the smell," said Lorraine.

Jarvis pulled himself up into the attic space and was immediately enveloped by a thick, unsettling darkness that seemed to swallow him whole. A sense of unease settled in the pit of his stomach, as he fumbled for his phone, desperately seeking the reassuring glow of its torch. When he finally managed to switch on the light, its beam cut through the murky shadows like a knife through fog, revealing a disarray of old bits of furniture draped in layers of dust, yellowing magazines from decades past, crumbling newspapers with faded headlines, and a few forlorn bags filled with moth-eaten clothes, that whispered tales of another time. As he moved cautiously further into the attic's depths, each creak and groan of the wooden beams beneath him resonated ominously in the silence.
He had to balance carefully as he navigated this forgotten space; it felt as if every step might awaken memories long buried or disturb something best left undisturbed. An unsettling feeling crept over him.... was he alone up here? The air was thick with an unnerving stillness, that made his heart race, as shadows danced around him in response to his movements. What secrets lay hidden among these relics?
As Jarvis cautiously made his way to the far end of the attic, a sense of dread settled over him like a heavy blanket. He navigated around a large, imposing wardrobe, its dark wood seeming almost ominous in the dim light. It was there that he discovered Blythe, slumped lifelessly against the wardrobe door, an unsettling sight that sent chills racing down his spine. The vacant stare of Blythe's eyes, wide open yet utterly devoid of life, seemed to gaze into an abyss beyond comprehension. It became painfully clear, that he had been dead for long enough, for the air in this cramped space to be thick with this unbearable stench.

A horrific blend of bodily decay and something far more rancid. The moment Jarvis took in the scene before him, he felt as if he were suffocating under the weight of reality; Blythe's body had lost all semblance of human dignity in death. His arm remained outstretched, a ghastly testament to his final moments, an image forever etched into Jarvis's mind. A rubber tube was tied tightly around hid arm, evidence of his desperate attempts to escape whatever demons had plagued him in life. A needle dangled precariously from where it had once injected substances into his veins…. substances that were now hauntingly ambiguous, but clearly lethal. The grim conclusion loomed over Jarvis: this last act was not merely one of indulgence, but rather likely the tragic culmination of an overdose, that had extinguished what little flicker of hope remained within Blythe's tortured exitance

.

Katrina

Jarvis felt an overwhelming sense of empathy for Katrina, as he prepared himself for the heart-wrenching duty of informing her, that her beloved brother had tragically passed away from an overdose. In a world filled with perilous pursuits, where they were relentlessly tracking him down …. either to exact revenge or to inflict suffering… his death now stood as a sobering reminder of the fragility of life. It was a senseless loss, stemming from what could easily be seen as a foolish decision, yet it was likely more akin to an unfortunate accident, rather than a deliberate choice.

As Jarvis steeled himself for this conversation, he couldn't help but reflect on the profound grief, that would engulf Katrina upon hearing such devastating news. He understood that this moment would irrevocably change her life, thrusting her into a whirlwind of sorrow and confusion as she grappled with the reality of losing someone so dear to her heart.

"Any luck, Jarvis?" asked McMatters. Jarvis looked at him, and McMatters knew; Jarvis didn't need to say anything more.

"Help me back down please Steve?" Jarvis asked.

Jarvis perched precariously on the edge of the hatch, his fingers gently gripping the old wooden rim as he dangled his legs over the side, feeling a mix of anxiety and anticipation. The world below him seemed both distant and daunting, yet there was a sense of trust in McMatters, who stood nearby with an encouraging presence, skilfully guiding him to a safe spot where he could leap down without fear. As Jarvis finally gathered the courage to make his descent, he felt a heavy weight settle in his chest. He walked slowly over to Katrina, his future wife, whose radiant spirit had always been a source of comfort and strength for him. However, in that moment, his face bore an expression filled with sadness and empathy; it was as though he could feel the gravity of their shared future pressing down on him.

"Katrina, I'm sorry... It's your brother; he's dead," said Jarvis softly.

At first, Katrina remained utterly motionless, her body frozen in place, as a profound stillness enveloped her. Her face bore no expression, and her heart felt heavy with an overwhelming tide of emotion, that surged within her like a stormy sea. The words she had just heard played over and over in her mind, echoing relentlessly and leaving her in a state of disbelief. Yes, she had harboured thoughts of wanting to kill the little bastard; after all, he had nearly brought about her own demise through his reckless actions.
Yet beneath that anger, lay the undeniable bond of family, she still loved him despite everything.
Now, however, he was gone... no longer burdened by pain or suffering. A bittersweet sense of relief washed over Katrina at the realisation, that he wouldn't have to endure any further agony; it was comforting to know that his passing had been swift and merciful. Still, the ache in her heart grew more profound as she grappled with the reality: he was not just

anyone; he was her brother. The complexity of their relationship intertwined love with frustration, a tumultuous mix that only siblings can truly understand. As an hour slipped by like sand through an hourglass, Katrina found herself unable to contain the flood of emotions any longer. She wept silently, tears cascading down her cheeks like gentle rain falling on parched earth… the silent testimony to both loss and love as she mourned the brother she would forever miss.

Chapter Forty-Five
The Shopping centre

When they finally reached the ground floor with the dog in tow, its discomfort became palpable; it started whining almost immediately. Recognising the signs of agitation, PC Jones promptly loosened the leash, allowing the animal more freedom to express itself. This dog is trained as a highly specialised cadaver dog, which means it possesses an innate ability to detect human remains without needing explicit commands. Instead, it springs into action at the slightest hint of a scent and requires nothing more than generous praise and treats when it successfully identifies its target. As they manoeuvred through the eerily quiet corridors of Debenhams' derelict shop, the dog's keen instincts kicked in.

It began sniffing with an intensity, that was hard to ignore, leading them deeper into what felt like a ghostly space, filled with remnants of consumerism long abandoned. With each step closer to the lift, its whines escalated, becoming increasingly urgent and anxious. Upon reaching the lift doors, the dog's behaviour shifted dramatically; it began frantically scratching at them as if trying to claw its way through. The urgency in its whines heightened further, creating an atmosphere thick with tension and anticipation as both PC Jones and his canine companion sensed that they were on the brink of uncovering something significant.

"You go and sort out the dog please?" Instructed Detective Winters.

"Good boy, come here, let's play," said PC Jones, as he guided the dog away from the lift and gave him the praise he deserved.

Detective Winters phoned the crime scene team, who were en route. "Extend the area; the dog has just found something on the ground floor inside the lift. You'll need to force the door open."

Detective Winters took a moment to gather her thoughts and assess the situation around her. It had been an exhaustingly long day, filled with relentless searching, each step taken in pursuit of leads, that seemed to slip through her fingers like sand. As the adrenaline gradually wore off, she became acutely aware of the gnawing hunger in her stomach and the parched sensation in her throat, that signalled a pressing need for hydration.

The once invigorating rush that had propelled her through hours of investigation now faded, leaving behind a stark reminder of her physical limitations. She could almost taste the dusty dryness on her tongue, urging her to refocus…. not just on the case at hand, but also on her own well-being.

A persistent question echoed relentlessly in the back of her mind: "how on earth did the child manage to see the body?" It seemed almost impossible, given the circumstances. From the vantage point of the third floor, visibility was severely limited; any view of what lay below was obstructed by walls and angles. The second floor, shrouded in mystery with its closed-off access, offered no opportunity for a glimpse either. Furthermore, the ground floor was entirely off-limits as well. It was as if an impenetrable barrier had been erected between her and answers she desperately sought, a baffling puzzle that left her questioning not only what she knew but also how a young child could have witnessed something so shocking from such confined spaces. Did he see who did it? Detective Winters needed to speak to that child, quickly.

"PC Steele can you see if the child is still at the station, please?" asked Detective Winters.

"I will check now." PC Steele left the area, hoping to find the child.

The Station

Detective Winters' team stood impatiently outside the Debenhams shop in the old Shopping centre; their anticipation palpable as they awaited the completion of the

162

forensic team's meticulous examination. The atmosphere was thick with tension; it had been an exceptionally long day for Winters, who had already endured a gruelling twelve-hour shift. Recognising the fatigue in her team, she had made the decision to send them off to clock out for some much-needed rest. Yet now, as she lingered on site…just moments away from her own opportunity to clock off.

Detective Winters found herself questioning that choice to linger. Her mind raced with thoughts of the demanding case, that had consumed them all and the mounting pressure to deliver results. In her determination to push through and maintain momentum, she had neglected her own basic needs; hunger gnawed at her stomach like a persistent ache, while a parched throat reminded her of her oversight regarding hydration. The consequences of prioritising work over self-care loomed larger than ever; not only was she feeling fatigued and drained, but clarity of thought was beginning to slip away.

In this high-stakes environment where every detail mattered tremendously, Detective Winters realised, that ignoring such fundamental necessities could result a clouding of her judgement at a critical juncture in their investigation. It became increasingly clear, that even a detective seasoned by experience must heed their body's signals and not simply for personal well-being, but also for effectiveness in solving crimes, that demanded unwavering focus and sharp analytical skills.

As she scanned the bustling scene around her…colleagues working diligently amidst scattered evidence, Winters resolved then and there not only to replenish herself physically, but also to foster an environment where self-care was valued just as much as relentless pursuit of justice. After all, even those who seek truth must first honour their own health, if they wish to succeed in unravelling complex mysteries lurking just beneath the surface.

Detective Winters stood on the edge of the crime scene, her attire a dishevelled mess from the relentless dust and dirt she had trudged through in her relentless pursuit of the truth. The grime clung to her like a second skin, a testament to the hours she had spent meticulously sifting through evidence and navigating the treacherous terrain surrounding this mysterious body. Each speck of dirt seemed to weigh heavily on her, not just physically but also symbolically; it served as a reminder of the grim reality she was confronting. As she surveyed the scene one last time, an overwhelming wave of fatigue washed over her.

It was clear, that if she wanted to maintain any semblance of clarity and focus for tomorrow's investigation, she would need to prioritise some much-needed self-care. She knew that returning home would provide her with an opportunity to cleanse not just her exterior, but also to recharge mentally and emotionally. A warm shower awaited her, promising to wash away both dirt and doubt, while a nourishing meal would fuel her for another day filled with challenging questions and complex puzzles.

Detective Winters made up her mind: she would head home, refresh herself thoroughly... because tomorrow's challenges required not only determination, but also renewed energy and clarity of thought if she was truly going to crack this case wide open.

"Hi Stacey, are you and your team OK to finish off here without me?" asked Detective Winters.
"Oh yes, we will be here many hours yet. Get yourself home and rest," said the forensic boss.
"Thank you, Stacey."

Detective Winters found herself in a state of complete disarray, her mind clouded by fatigue and frustration. The weight of her unresolved cases had become an unbearable burden, sapping her focus and clarity. With every passing moment in the precinct, the once vibrant passion that had propelled her into this line of work, was slowly being eclipsed by exhaustion. Realising that she could no longer function effectively under such circumstances, she made the difficult decision to leave the office behind for the day. As she stepped outside into the crisp evening air, a sense of relief washed over her; it was time to seek solace in the comfort of home and allow herself a much-needed reprieve from the relentless demands of her job.

Chapter Forty-Six
A call to make

Katrina was taken aback by the profound weight of the words spoken by Jarvis. The impact of each syllable hung in the air like a heavy fog, leaving her feeling numb and adrift, unsure of how to respond, or what course of action to take in that moment of unbearable grief. Her mind raced as she grappled with the stark reality, that her brother was dead. Yes, there had been times when she had felt an overwhelming desire to end his life…. a sentiment born from their tumultuous history and fractured relationship…. but this was an entirely different scenario.

For Katrina, taking such drastic action would have been a dark and almost straightforward resolution to her suffering; however, for her brother to die from an overdose….an unintentional act wrought with despair, that was something far more tragic and complex. This loss not only shattered her world, but also forced her to confront feelings of guilt and regret, that clawed at her heart like a relentless tide, leaving behind echoes of what could have been…. if only circumstances had played out differently.

"Katrina, we need to call the police and let them handle it," said Lorraine.
"I agree, Lorraine, but we can't be here," said McMatters.
"It will be a long, drawn-out process if we stay, and if they suspect any wrongdoing, we'll be the first they take prints from," said Jarvis.
"That won't be a wise move," said McMatters.
"I'll ring them and say I think someone is dead up there in the attic because of the smell, and that I need someone to check," said Katrina.
"Are you sure, Katrina?" asked Lorraine.
"Yes, you all go back to the club. I'll meet you there," said Katrina.

Katrina, although she harboured a deep-seated reluctance to embrace solitude, recognised that she required some time and space to reflect on and process the tumultuous events, that had recently unfolded in her life. The whirlwind of emotions swirling within her…. confusion and sadness. Katrina waited until they had gone before calling the police.

"999, what's your emergency?"
"I think someone, possibly my brother, might be dead in the attic. There's a really bad smell," said Katrina.
"Are you at the house now?"
"Yes."
"I'll just gather some details from you, then send some officers out." They took all Katrina's details and details of her brother, where she thought he was and why, where she was… far too many questions Katrina just wanted this over and done with.

Katrina mechanically went through the motions of providing the address, each word feeling like a weight pressing down on her. The officers had asked her to step out of the house and wait for their arrival outside, which only heightened her sense of unease. She felt a knot tightening in her stomach at the thought of sharing her personal details, especially with the police…figures that often-represented authority and scrutiny, which she found particularly intimidating. In that moment, she was engulfed by an overwhelming desire to retreat into the safety of her own space. The prospect of engaging with them felt burdensome and exhausting; she simply did not want to confront whatever questions or procedures awaited her just outside the door.
It took twenty minutes for any police officers to arrive. Katrina repeated everything again, explaining that she had come looking for her brother, because no one had seen him.

"When did you last see your brother?" asked PC Maylan.

"Ummm, five to seven days ago. It could have been more, though," Katrina guessed, as she couldn't think straight.
"And whereabouts is the smell?"
"It hits you when you open the door, then gets stronger near the attic hatch. I checked all the rooms for him, but no luck. I can't reach the attic."
"OK, stay there while we go inside and check," said PC Maylan.

Katrina nodded slowly, her heart heavy with an overwhelming weight, that seemed to press down on her chest, consuming her from the inside out. The reality of the situation loomed over her like a dark cloud, suffocating and relentless.
Yet, despite the turmoil swirling within her, she held back the tears that threatened to spill over. She knew she couldn't allow herself to cry just yet. Not until they had confirmed he was dead…. until there was undeniable proof of his death.

Searching for the Body

PC Maylan and PC Jones had taken a brief statement from Katrina Garcia, a task that had already begun to weigh heavily on their hearts. Now, as they step across the threshold and enter the property, they are immediately confronted by a powerful, nauseating waft, that hits them square in the face with an almost palpable force. It is an overwhelming stench…. rotten and sickening…. that engulfs their senses, forcing them to gag repeatedly as their stomachs churn in protest. This foul odour seems to hang thickly in the air, an unwelcome reminder of neglect and decay, that lingers long after it first strikes.
The officers exchange troubled glances, acutely aware that this moment is not just about the physical discomfort caused by the smell; it also serves as a stark indicator of deeper

168

issues at play within these walls…. a haunting reflection of despair, that resonates far beyond its noxious scent.

The officers exchange solemn nods, a silent agreement passing between them as they acknowledge the unsettling scent that permeates the air…. a tell-tale sign of death. However, at this stage in their investigation, it remains unclear whether the source of this distressing odour belongs to an animal or a human; both carry a unique and unmistakable aroma, that lingers with the senses long after it's encountered. With heavy hearts and focused minds, PC Jones and PC Maylan begin their methodical search, moving from room to room with purpose. The absence of furniture allows for unhindered passage through the dimly lit space, making their task somewhat easier as they navigate each area with careful consideration. Each step taken echoes softly in the stillness, heightening the tension that surrounds them as they seek answers.

They finally reach the dimly lit stairway under the attic hatch. As soon as PC Maylan steps into this area of the house, he feels an overwhelming wave of nausea wash over him. The relentless gagging becomes too much to bear, and despite his best efforts to maintain control, he finds himself, unable to hold back the surge. In a moment of desperation, PC Jones begins scanning the cluttered surroundings for something…. anything….to climb on to reach the attic. PC Jones heads down to the back garden in search of a box, step, or ladder. He finds a solid box that might help him reach into the attic space. PC Jones takes a deep breath of fresh air before venturing back inside to the overpowering odour.

The attic is strewn with forgotten relics from years past; old furniture draped in white sheets and boxes overflowing with memories long abandoned. It is then that a chilling thought crosses their mind: if there's truly something dead in this musty space, it must be substantial enough, that it couldn't possibly have just wandered up here on its own. What kind of creature could manage such a feat? The mere idea sends shivers down their spine as they grapple with both fear and curiosity about what lies hidden among these shadows. Tucked away behind a large, imposing wardrobe is a man who appears to be trapped in a nightmarish state, with a needle still embedded in his arm and his eyes staring blankly into the void, devoid of any life or recognition. The sight is harrowing, an unsettling reminder of the depths to which some individuals can fall when engulfed by addiction. PC Jones, confronted with this tragic scene for the first time, was unable to contain himself and was the first to succumb to the overwhelming horror of it all, retching violently as he processed what lay before him. Not long after, PC Maylan felt the same gut-wrenching sensation take hold of him; it was as if their bodies could not reconcile the reality of such despair. The air around them was thick with an oppressive heaviness…. a musty blend of dust and decay, that clung stubbornly to their senses. With nowhere for the acrid smell to escape, it lingered like an unwelcome spectre in that dimly lit room, amplifying the sense of hopelessness that permeated this grim tableau.

They called in the forensic team more as a formality, rather than out of any genuine suspicion of wrongdoing, and stepped outside into the open air. The moment they crossed the threshold, they were greeted by a gentle breeze, that wrapped around them like a comforting embrace, offering not just fresh air, but also a brief respite from the heavy atmosphere inside. As they inhaled deeply, their senses welcomed the crispness of nature; it was as if each breath helped to wash away the remnants of the unsettling scents that lingered in their nostrils.

"Miss Gacia, we have confirmed there is a body in the attic. At this stage, I can't say if it is your brother, but as this is his house, it's quite likely," said PC Maylan.
"Oh, no, please no, but how?" asked Katrina.

"It looks like an overdose. Would you like me to call someone to come get you?" inquired PC Jones, as tears silently fell down her face.

"No, but thank you."

"As soon as we know more, we will contact you, Miss Gacia," said PC Maylan.

Chapter Forty-Seven
Maxine

Maxine had been off gallivanting with Demetrio for what felt like four months, or was it five? Honestly, time had become as slippery as a greased pig at a country fair; she was having so much fun, that the days seemed to vanish. Yet, during her sun-soaked adventures and culinary escapades, she couldn't shake off the pang of missing her daughter. More importantly, she found herself yearning for the baby bump, that was now taking centre stage in her daughter Lorraine's life. It wouldn't be long before little feet would be pattering about, and Maxine wanted to be there to witness all those toe-curling, heart-melting moments. A chance to right a wrong from her past …. a golden opportunity to fix what she got so badly wrong. It's as if life had handed her the ultimate do-over. This time, she could finally set the record straight and sprinkle some much-needed fairy dust on those previous missteps. Imagine her joy as she realises that she can fix her own mistakes.

Meanwhile, Demetrio had been working his fingers to the bone at his family's restaurant…. if he kept going like this, he'd earn himself an honorary degree in juggling pots and pans! But alas, reality loomed on the horizon like an overzealous parent at a school play; their time away from home was ending. Maxine found herself torn between her newfound love for this charming place, that had nestled itself into her heart like an overly affectionate cat and the undeniable tug of family responsibilities pulling her back. She would miss this slice of paradise where every day felt like an episode of a rom-com…. but let's face it, no one could resist the allure of returning home where hugs were plentiful and baby snuggles awaited!

Maxine had picked the phone up and put it down more times than she could count, but with a deep breath she called her daughter.

"Hi Mum, how is Italy today?" said Lorraine.

"It's lovely and wonderful; this place is magical," said Maxine.

"Why do I sense a 'but'?"

"I miss home and the bump... I bet you have a nice tidy bump now, and I'm not there," Maxine sobbed, struggling to keep her emotions in check.

"Oh, Mum... You will be back before you know it. Does Demetrio know you miss home?"

"No, he's got enough to think about."

"Tell him, Mum, he will understand."

"I... I don't know. I will think about it."

"Bump is doing fine, though, so don't worry."

"I want to be home before you have it. When are you going to find out if it's a boy or girl? It feels odd calling it 'the bump' or just 'it.'"

"Nope, it will be a surprise, but I feel we have a kick-arse girl. However, Steve thinks the strong kicks are from a boy."

"I'm not sure how, but you normally know what you're having. It's strange, but you feel it."

"Yes, I feel it's a girl."

Maxine squealed in delight; there was no way she was going to miss her daughter's baby being born without being there. She hadn't been there all her life because of drinking or men, but no more. She knew she needed to talk with Demetrio and just hoped he felt the same.

"I need to go, Mum, but we will talk soon. Let me know what Demetrio says."

"Will do. Bye, Lorraine."

Chapter Forty-Eight
The Funeral

Katrina decided to organise a modest funeral without a formal service, knowing that Blythe had never been one for religious practices and would have felt uncomfortable in a church or chapel. Instead, she envisioned a small gathering at the burial site, where those close to him could share their memories and pay respects in an intimate setting. A few heartfelt words were to be spoken, allowing everyone present to reflect on Blythe's life and his impact on them. Following this simple yet meaningful ceremony, there would be an opportunity for friends and family to gather over drinks at Dreams. This location was suitable as it did not open on Mondays, ensuring the occasion could be held in a peaceful atmosphere without the usual hustle and bustle. It allowed for an undisturbed remembrance, where stories could be exchanged, laughter mingled with tears, and cherished memories of Blythe celebrated among those who loved him most.

All of Blythe's friends and acquaintances, including the Santos and the Bennetts, attended the gathering at Dreams, and it was fortunate the venue was spacious enough for everyone. The atmosphere was warm, as Blythe's old crew arrived to pay their respects, reminding everyone of the bonds they had shared over the years. Lorraine and Paulie went above and beyond by arranging an impressive food spread, catering to various tastes, ensuring no one went hungry during this poignant occasion. Among the delightful offerings stood a cake, that Katrina remarked was particularly fitting for her brother; it captured his essence beautifully. The cake was not merely a dessert, but an artistic representation shaped like a bomb, complete with intricate details, that brought smiles while evoking fond memories. As guests gathered around, they couldn't help but comment on its striking design; it sparked stories and laughter amidst reflection, as they all shared in both grief and celebration for Blythe.

It wasn't until after the gathering at Dreams, when only she and Jarvis were left alone in the quiet aftermath, that the full weight of her loss crashed down upon Katrina. In that hushed moment, reality truly set in: her brother was not just away; he was dead, gone forever. The enormity of this truth enveloped her like a cold shroud, and she shuddered involuntarily as waves of sorrow washed over her.

Tears began to stream down her face relentlessly, each drop carrying fragments of memories... laughter shared, secrets whispered during late-night conversations, and moments that now felt achingly distant. Finally allowing herself this release, she wept continuously, pouring out all the pent-up grief, that had remained trapped inside her heart for too long. In this vulnerable state, she began to confront the profound sense of loss for her brother... a realisation that would take time to accept, but was essential for healing.

Chapter Forty-Nine
The Club

McMatters and Lorraine had been diligently keeping the club running smoothly, while simultaneously managing the needs of the families involved, a task that often felt both rewarding and challenging. During this time, Jarvis dedicated his efforts to assisting Katrina, ensuring that she was supported in her endeavours. The families associated with the club were incredibly cooperative and understanding, each one readily offering a helping hand whenever necessary, especially given Lorraine's visible pregnancy. Their kindness created a warm atmosphere of camaraderie, that further strengthened their bond. One particularly thoughtful gesture came from Paulie, who had ingeniously transformed Lorraine's beloved cocktail decanter into a delightful mocktail drink. This creative adaptation brought Lorraine immense joy; she found it just as delicious and satisfying as the real thing, allowing her to indulge without any concerns during her pregnancy.

On this day, Jarvis and Katrina were scheduled to return to the club after their time away. Though McMatters reassured them that there was no urgent need for them to rush back, both Jarvis and Katrina expressed a strong desire to stay engaged and busy with their responsibilities. McMatters completely understood this need for occupation; he recognised how important it was for them to feel involved and purposeful during such a transitional period. However, amidst all this business, loomed McMatter's concern for Lorraine's wellbeing. Given past events that had cast shadows over their line of work…. along with his protective instincts…. he worried about her venturing out alone without sufficient support.

Today marked an important transition, as Katrina began taking over some of Lorraine's duties at the club. She was eager to learn the ropes, so that Lorraine could take some well-deserved time to relax more fully. At five months along in her pregnancy, with much still left unfinished on the nursery front, Lorraine looked forward with great anticipation to completing it before welcoming her new arrival into the world.... a project infused with love and dreams for what lay ahead.

"Here they are, welcome back, you two," said Lorraine as Jarvis and Katrina walked into the office.
"It's good to be back. I need to keep busy," said Katrina.
"Come, we'll grab a drink, and I'll fill you in on where we're up to." said Lorraine.

While Katrina and Lorraine ventured off to immerse themselves in the details of Blythe's old empire ....an empire that would soon transition into Katrina's stewardship.... McMatters and Jarvis seized the opportunity to catch up on recent developments. Jarvis felt a sense of satisfaction as he noted how the families had taken the initiative, stepping up to address and resolve any issues that had arisen within their ranks. It was heartening to see such proactive engagement, demonstrating a commitment to collaboration and stability during this transitional phase. All McMatters requested was to be kept informed about any significant changes or updates as they unfolded. This approach not only reassured him, but also promised to make Jarvis's life considerably easier, while Katrina acclimatised herself to her new role within the business.... a role that came with its own set of challenges, along with opportunities for growth.
McMatters and Jarvis had never truly viewed the empire they meticulously built as reminiscent of a mafia organisation, but upon reflecting on the intricate structure of their business, they began to see the parallels more clearly. It was a fascinating revelation: they were, in essence, one large family, albeit one intricately divided into smaller segments.... each representing distinct families, that skilfully managed various aspects of the enterprise. In this unique arrangement,

each boss held command over a dedicated team, fostering an environment in which collaboration flourished.

What struck McMatters most was how remarkably refreshing it was that everyone within this expansive network genuinely got along. They worked together seamlessly, offering help and support to one another without a moment's hesitation, or thought for personal gain. It created an atmosphere of camaraderie, that infused the workplace with energy and motivation. McMatters had never imagined it would evolve in such a harmonious manner. He had initially envisioned himself merely as a club owner who took no nonsense from anyone. Meanwhile, Jarvis stood firmly by his side, as his partner in crime…. together navigating both challenges and triumphs with unwavering loyalty and shared purpose. This unexpected sense of unity made them realise, that they had cultivated not just a successful business, but also an enduring familial bond within its structure.

Now, he was on the midst of becoming a father, a milestone that had long been a cherished dream of his. The anticipation swelled within him, an exhilarating mix of excitement and nervousness. Just as life often unfolds in unexpected ways, Lorraine entered his world like a whirlwind, her vibrant energy and warmth transforming it in ways he had never imagined possible. With her presence came an array of changes…. both profound and delightful, that enriched his life far beyond what he could have anticipated. The thought of meeting his own child filled him with joy and wonder; he could hardly contain himself as he envisioned holding this tiny being in his arms, sharing moments that would forever shape their lives together.

"OK, Lorraine and Steve, go take some time, maybe get that nursery finished. We've got this place covered," said Jarvis. "Thanks, mate," said McMatters.

Chapter Fifty
Results

Detective Winters stood at her desk, a picture of calm determination as she patiently awaited the return of Stacey, the forensic team leader. She had been informed, that an update regarding the shopping centre investigation was imminent. But the lengthy wait had begun to fray her nerves. The process was taking longer than usual, largely due to the sheer volume and complexity of evidence, that needed meticulous examination. Stacey's time was precious; she had a critical meeting scheduled in just thirty minutes. Winters felt a deep sense of urgency; any scrap of information, no matter how seemingly insignificant, could prove invaluable in piecing together this intricate puzzle.

The weight of responsibility rested heavily on her shoulders.... ever since she had taken over from Jackson, whom many considered a seasoned detective with an impressive track record, she had faced immense pressure to deliver results. It was disheartening, that not one single case had been successfully solved during her tenure thus far.... this lingering failure gnawed at her conscience and made each passing day feel like another insurmountable challenge.
As she cast her gaze through the office window into the bustling corridor outside, Winters spotted Stacey making her way towards her office. However, what caught Winters' attention was not just Stacey's presence, but rather how she appeared to pause three times along the route, before finally reaching Detective Winters' door. Each stop seemed deliberate and laden with unspoken tension; it piqued Winters' curiosity about what news would emerge from their impending discussion and whether it might finally provide a breakthrough in what had become an exceedingly frustrating string of unsolved cases.

"Good morning, Detective Winters," said Stacey, bright and bubbly.

"Morning Stacey. I'm worn out this morning" said Detective Winters.

"Well, I have news! The Shopping centre had many footprints, which was a waste of time, but from what I have worked out, someone on the third floor was dragged backwards on a chair. So, I'm guessing they were tied to the chair at some point. It seems it was used to extract information from that person, and it looks like that's the same person we found at the bottom of the lift shaft. Although no sign of the rope was found," said Stacey.

"What about the bowl?" asked Detective Winters.

"The bowl seems to have been used to torture the same person, due to the markings found on their feet and ankles. There's no ID on the body, so we still have no name, as they're not in the system," said Stacey.

"I was hoping for a break. I need to solve something," said Detective Winters.

"Well, I do have something interesting. I found three partial prints, not in the system, but they do partially match other things."

"You do like to tease me, don't you?"

"The pub and the Shopping centre share a partial print. A different print matches one on another body, the one left in the street for everyone to see, and the third matches a weapon found at a third crime scene."

"Blimey."

"Now, here's where it gets interesting: a match was flagged from a different lab on the other side of town, that matches all three crime scenes."

"Wow, I wasn't expecting I could clean up and finally solve three crime scenes. That's amazing."

"Not so quick. Yes, you may be able to solve them, but the prints match a dead man. He died well over two months ago, almost three months in fact."

"How did he die?"

"An overdose. He took a cocktail of amphetamines and heroin. Other drugs found in his system included crack and LSD. This guy didn't want to wake up."

"What's his name?"

"Hevran Blythe."

"Oh yes, Jones and Maylan were on that case. His sister couldn't locate him and found his house had a rotting odour, so she called us in. Thanks, Stacey. I can wrap up three cases. I feel so much better now."

"You're welcome." Stacey hands over the file on all her findings and heads back to the lab.

Detective Winters was absolutely over the moon; at long last, the disparate pieces of the intricate puzzle had aligned perfectly, allowing her to unravel and solve not just one, but three different cases that had been plaguing her for weeks. The thrill of connecting the dots, filled her with an exhilarating sense of accomplishment. It was as if all her hard work, late nights poring over evidence, and countless hours spent interviewing witnesses had culminated in this triumphant moment.

What a wonderfully great day this was! The sun shone brightly outside her office window, mirroring the joy bubbling inside her, as she reflected on how satisfying it felt to bring closure to these mysteries, that had eluded resolution for so long. Each solved case represented not just a professional victory, but also a personal one…. justice served and lives positively impacted.

Detective Winters couldn't wait to share the completed case files with the team and give them to Sergeant Cole.

Chapter Fifty-One
The Nursery

McMatters and Lorraine were having an absolute riot, as they playfully painted the nursery, both looking like modern-day Picassos covered in splashes of paint, that could rival a chaotic art exhibit, a bit like one of Lorraine's blood splatters. They had decided on a cheerful pastel yellow and crisp white, perfect for creating a serene environment…. ideal for when their little one arrives and decides to make their grand entrance into the world. However, this delightful colour scheme was merely a temporary affair; once the baby reached the ripe old age of toddlerhood (which is basically when they start throwing tantrums), McMatters and Lorraine would embark on an adventurous quest to select a new colour, that perfectly matched their child's budding personality….be it fiery red for a little diva or cool blue for a future philosopher. Who knew painting could turn into such an entertaining spectacle? With every brushstroke, they not only transformed the walls, but also inadvertently created abstract art on each other's faces, proving that parenting starts with a good dose of humour and creativity!

With just three months left until the big day, time was flying by at a pace, that would make a jet fighter envious. The baby furniture had already made its grand entrance into the soon-to-be nursery, occupying every spare inch of space like an uninvited guest who refuses to leave. McMatters had quickly learned, that his fiancée possessed quite the talent for wielding a screwdriver, effortlessly assembling cribs and changing tables with the finesse of a seasoned carpenter. However, when it came to using a hammer, well, let's just say it was akin to watching a cat trying to swim…. amusing and slightly terrifying all at once. The last time she took on that task, not only did several nails end up bent beyond recognition, but their wall also bore witness to what could only be described as abstract art in the form of random holes and questionable dents. McMatters quickly covered up the evidence from the hammer and painted over it.

Just one more trip was required to complete the grand scavenger hunt, known colloquially as preparing for a baby. This mission involved filling up the changing unit with an impressive array of nappies, wipes, and enough baby lotions to make a spa jealous. They also had to gather some basic clothes.... because let's face it, the little one can't just be swaddled in nothing but dreams and hopes!

With just a pram and a car seat left to buy, it's as if they're on the last lap of a very peculiar race, where the prize is parenthood and possibly a lifetime supply of baby wipes. It's almost like these purchases require an Olympic-level decision-making process. Do they go for the sleek, high-tech pram, that practically folds itself, or opt for one that looks like it could survive an asteroid impact? And what about the car seat? Should they choose one, that promises safety ratings so high they could send an astronaut to Mars in it, or one that's just as comfy as your favourite armchair, but can withstand a toddler's snack attack?

It was starting to get a bit freaky, like something out of a low-budget horror film. Lorraine, with all the confidence of a magician about to pull a rabbit out of a hat, grabbed his hand and firmly placed it on her belly. And just when you thought things couldn't get weirder.... boom! McMatter's hand seemed to launch itself from her belly like an overzealous jack-in-the-box, springing forth as if he were auditioning for a role in an action movie. The look on his face was priceless; one part shock, two parts absolute bewilderment! You could practically hear the dramatic film score swelling in the background, as he processed what had just happened. It was the sort of moment, that makes you question your life choices, while simultaneously wondering if you should be reaching for the popcorn instead of your partner's hand!

183

"Wow, that was some kick. I had felt little bits of movement, but that's something else." McMatters was surprised. It was a weird feeling, when you feel a foot pop out of the skin.
"Yes, now you know why I'm not sleeping for long. I get booted all night."
"We must be having a boy with that kick."
"I still feel it's a she, and she kicks arse, just like her mummy... oh wow, now I've said it, it feels odd."
"I know what you mean. I have to keep pinching myself to make sure I'm not dreaming."

Chapter Fifty-Two
Demetrio

After Maxine had expressed her desire to return home, Demetrio found himself engulfed in a whirlwind of emotions, that left him feeling uncertain. They had spent an incredible six months and three weeks in charming Italy, where their efforts had been devoted to revitalising his family's beloved restaurant. The once struggling establishment was now buzzing with life, the staff were radiating happiness, and his family couldn't have been more grateful for the support they received during this challenging time.

With the restaurant back on its feet and operating smoothly, it became clear that their mission was accomplished. Despite the beauty of Italy…. the breath-taking landscapes, the rich culture, and the warmth of its people, Demetrio felt a strong pull towards home. He was eager to return and check on his own restaurant, wanting to ensure everything was still running as it should be. The quaint charm of his hometown held a special place in his heart; however, above all else, it was Maxine who truly captured his affections.
To Demetrio, her presence far outweighed any other consideration or attachment he had developed during their time abroad. With determination coursing through him, like an Italian espresso racing through his veins, Demetrio sat down with his family to discuss the next steps.

Together they decided it was time for them to take back control of the restaurant operations, while ensuring everything would continue smoothly without him at the helm for a while. Once he felt confident, that everything was set in place, they would head back home. Demetrio turned to Maxine with excitement bubbling within him, as he prepared to share this new chapter of their lives together.

"Maxine, I know it's been a few weeks since you said you wanted to go back home. As you know, it couldn't be an instant thing, because I had to show them how to run the restaurant, so it doesn't get as bad as it was when we first arrived. Maxine, do you still want to go home?"

"Oh, Demetrio, yes I do."

"Well, let's pack. I have a flight booked for two weeks' time, but don't tell anyone... let's surprise them and shower them with gifts."

"Yes, oh what a wonderful idea, Demetrio! Can we go get the gifts today?"

"Yes." Demetrio chuckled as the bubbly Maxine came alive at the thought of going home.

While Maxine went to get her self ready, Demetrio popped outside and made a call to McMatters. He'd need his help.

"Hello," said McMatters.

"Steve, it's Demetrio."

"Oh, hello Demetrio, how are you?"

"I'm great, thank you. I need your help."

"What do you need? You know I will always help."

"We are coming home in two weeks. We want to surprise Lorraine. Could you arrange transport to collect us from the airport, please?"

"Consider it done. Send me the flight details, and don't worry, I won't say a word."

"Thank you, Steve, I appreciate it so much."

"You're welcome."

"Got to go, Maxine's coming. Talk soon."

"Bye, Demetrio."

Another thing off the list. Demetrio knew he still had a lot to sort out before they went home.

Chapter Fifty-Three
Detective Winters

Detective Winters was seated at her desk, having recently completed the meticulous reports concerning three pivotal incidents: the troubling situation at the Shopping centre, the unfortunate case of a drug overdose, and the discovery of a weapon concealed in a narrow alleyway. The successful resolution of these interconnected cases, simultaneously marked a significant milestone in her career. It represented, not only her dedication to duty, but also an unexpected yet much-needed stroke of luck amidst the often-unpredictable nature of police work. Detective Winters read it through one last time before she took it up to Sergeant Cole.

"The weapon located in the alleyway was unearthed by an observant member of the public, who promptly reported the find to the authorities. Subsequently, it was collected by Police Constable Maitland, who ensured that proper protocol was followed during this critical phase of investigation. Following the retrieval of the firearm, a meticulous forensic dusting operation was conducted by Stacey, the head of the forensic team renowned for her expertise and precision in such matters.

Upon completing her examination, she concluded, that two partial fingerprints had been identified: one situated on the magazine and another present on the barrel chamber. However, despite thorough searches through all existing databases, it was determined that no matches could be found for these prints within any current files. This lack of correspondence raised significant questions regarding potential suspects and highlights a gap in available evidence, that may impede further investigative efforts.

The Shopping centre: an extensive search operation was instigated following a concerning report made by a child, which indicated potential criminal activity within the vicinity.

Regrettably, amidst the efforts to locate the child's whereabouts, after they had left the station, a significant error occurred, resulting in the child's details remaining unaccounted for. Nevertheless, during the thorough investigation of the Shopping centre's premises, crucial evidence was uncovered at a specific crime scene. The remains of an individual were discovered within the confines of what was once the old Debenhams department store. Investigators found significant evidence spread across both the third and first floors of this now-defunct retail space. On the third floor, authorities noted an unusual disturbance. A chair had been forcibly dragged across the room towards the lift shaft, revealing signs of a struggle or movement, that warranted further examination. Additionally, several items were located on this level.... a bowl and various electrical wires...which are believed to be linked to acts of torture; however, no fingerprints were retrieved from these items. On investigating further down on the first floor, a specially trained cadaver dog succeeded in locating human remains concealed within an elevator shaft.

This area proved particularly challenging for our forensic teams, as access had to be gained using hydraulic rescue tools known as "the jaws of life." Upon retrieval of the body from its precarious position within the shaft, investigators noted distinct signs indicating prior torture associated with electrical wires found nearby and evident trauma consistent with a severe fall from a considerable height. The circumstances suggest, that this individual had been forcibly thrown down into the lift shaft. Compounding this tragic discovery is that while initial forensic examinations did not yield any matches in our identification systems.... the body itself does not appear to be registered.... the forensic team did however, successfully recover a second fingerprint from a watch, that was affixed to one wrist. This detail may prove pivotal in corroborating identities, or uncovering vital information regarding this unfortunate incident as investigations continue unabated.

The Tragic Incident of Drug Overdose: On the scene of a distressing event, law enforcement officials reported the discovery of a deceased body. Police Constables Jones and Maylan arrived at the location, responding to a call for assistance from Katrina Gacia, who was anxiously searching for her brother.

Upon their arrival, they were met with an overwhelming and unpleasant odour, that filled the air, a harbinger of the grim reality that awaited them. Tragically, it was confirmed, that the individual found deceased in the attic, was indeed her brother, Hevran Blythe. Hevran's untimely demise resulted from what is commonly referred to as a lethal cocktail.... a combination of substances so potent that it led to his sudden death. In addition to this heart-wrenching revelation, further investigations revealed intriguing yet troubling details regarding Hevran's past. An autopsy was conducted which included fingerprint analysis.

Remarkably, his prints matched those collected from various crime scenes linked to incidents involving weapons, in both urban street environments and shopping centres. This connection raises significant questions about his involvement in potential criminal activities prior to his tragic overdose, painting a complex picture of an individual whose life ended prematurely amid troubling circumstances. So, I hereby close these three cases together as one, with all reports included from the other departments."

Detective Winters was absolutely elated at the prospect of successfully closing a considerable number of cases simultaneously. This remarkable achievement not only reflected her unwavering dedication and expertise in the field of criminal investigation, but also brought a sense of profound satisfaction to her professional endeavours. However, it was with a heavy heart, that she acknowledged the unresolved case concerning her predecessor, Detective Jackson. The lingering mystery surrounding his untimely demise weighed on her conscience, leaving an indelible mark on her thoughts. Yet, despite this setback, she remained optimistic and resolute in her belief that one day, through tenacity and relentless pursuit of justice, she would uncover the truth behind his murder and bring closure to that haunting chapter.

Detective Winters went upstairs to drop the files off with Wendy.

Chapter Fifty-Four
Lorraine

Lorraine wasn't feeling well; an unsettling sensation gnawed at her, an inexplicable discomfort, that she couldn't quite pinpoint. Deep down, however, something primal urged her to believe that it wasn't good. The familiar pangs of anxiety twisted in her stomach, as she contemplated her condition. Just to be certain, she decided to call the midwife for advice and reassurance. After all, Lorraine was due for her regular health checks anyway, so when the midwife agreed to come by for a visit, it felt like a prudent decision. Initially, Lorraine's worry was manageable.... she thought perhaps it was just a fleeting malaise, or fatigue from the long days leading up to this momentous occasion.

However, everything shifted when the midwife arrived accompanied by a doctor; that was when alarm bells began ringing in Lorraine's mind. It suddenly felt more serious than she had anticipated. The presence of medical professionals often evokes a sense of urgency and concern.... like clouds gathering before a storm. As they settled into the living room, Lorraine's heart raced with unease, while Susan quickly assessed the tension in the air and instinctively recognised Lorraine's worried expression.... a look that spoke volumes about her inner turmoil.

Without hesitation, Susan dashed off to phone Steve, knowing that whatever was happening required his support and presence, now more than ever. The weight of uncertainty hung heavily in the room, as they waited for answers and comfort amidst their growing anxiety.

"Hi Lorraine, let's take a look at you. We'll start with your blood pressure. Then, if you can, I need a urine sample. I'll listen to the baby and do an exam. Is that, OK?" said the midwife.

"Yes, that's fine, thank you," Lorraine replied.

"While Alison is doing all that, I need you to tell me what is happening," said the doctor.

"For a few days, I just haven't felt right...tired and weak. I seem to eat non-stop, but after eating, I get a dragging, pulling feeling that hurts," Lorraine explained.

"Can you show me where?" the doctor asked.

Lorraine pointed to the centre of her stomach, the midwife finished her job, and then she started to discuss the results with the doctor. Steve walked in as if he had just run from the car, kissed Lorraine, and then joined the doctor and midwife in the discussion, Steve came to her side and held her hand.

"OK," said the doctor, "We are admitting you into Hospital, so we can monitor you more closely. I want to know more about the feelings you're experiencing, and your blood pressure is high, so it's complete bed rest while on the baby monitor."

"I found proteins in your water, so I'd like to re-test at the hospital. Do you have your bag packed? It's possible you won't be out until after you've had the baby." said the midwife.

"I do, yes," said Lorraine.

Lorraine looked at Steve, uncertain and worried. This was not what she had expected, and she was unprepared for it.

"It's OK, I'll have the bags brought up later. Let's get you both to the hospital and safe," said McMatters.

McMatters nodded at Susan, because she knew what to do and whom to contact, but she wasn't aware of Lorraine's mum, who was due at the airport in two hours.

Steve went over to Susan and whispered so Lorraine couldn't hear, "Maxine and Demetrio are due at the airport in two hours. Transport is arranged for them to come here; it was a surprise! Can you fill them in on the situation and get them over to the hospital? Our driver will be on hand for this," said McMatters.

192

Susan nodded and handed Steve two bags. "Yellow is for the baby, purple is Lorraine's."

"Thank you, Susan," said McMatters.

Steve got Lorraine into the car and strapped her in; he didn't have time to think too much.

"Follow us, we will rush her through," said the doctor.

And rush the doctor did, blue lights flashing ferociously and the siren blazing a piercing wail, that sliced through the tension in the air. With determination etched on his face, Steve stayed close on the doctor's tail, his heart pounding in his chest like a war drum. As they sped through the chaotic scene, filled with anxious bystanders and swirling emotions, an overwhelming sense of dread settled in Steve's gut; he couldn't shake off the feeling, that they were teetering on the edge of something dire and unknown.

The Hospital

Once at the hospital, a sense of unease enveloped them, as they led Lorraine into a private room, situated just next to the bustling nurses' station. The atmosphere felt heavy with unspoken worries and anticipation. As they hooked her up to a drip, Steve couldn't help but feel a knot tightening in his stomach; this was all becoming all too real. They then attached the foetal monitor, which provided rhythmic beeping sounds, that were intended to reassure them about the little one's well-being, yet somehow it only magnified their anxiety. The medical staff proceeded to scan Lorraine's bump, their faces focused and professional, and kindly instructed them to look away if they did not wish to discover the gender of their baby just yet. Meanwhile, they inserted the cannula…. a precautionary measure, that further deepened their sense of dread about what might unfold in this sterile environment, filled with medical equipment and hushed conversations.

Maxine and Demetrio

Maxine and Demetrio stepped into the airport pick-up area; it was good to be home again. The familiarity of the space was comforting, but the whirlwind of events, that had led them here loomed large in their minds. Maxine felt an overwhelming sense of gratitude, that it hadn't been a long flight; the mere thought of enduring hours cramped in economy class sent a shiver down her spine. Instead, they had flown first class...a luxurious upgrade courtesy of McMatters, transforming what could have been a tedious journey, into an indulgent experience filled with exquisite meals and unparalleled comfort.

As they settled back into reality after their airborne escapade, they savoured a splendid meal served at 30,000 feet...an experience far removed from the usual bland airline fare. Rich flavours danced on their palates as they relished every bite, grateful for the culinary delight, that broke up the monotony of travel.

However, amidst her reflections on comfort and culinary excellence, Maxine's heart raced when she scanned the bustling arrivals area. She hadn't expected to see their names displayed prominently on any board welcoming them back home. A wave of relief washed over her, when she realised it was for them: 'Lorraine's driver' waiting patiently among the throng of family members and friends reuniting with loved ones. This small twist brought some calm to her racing thoughts, reminding her they were finally back where they belonged, even amidst ongoing uncertainty.

"Does Lorraine know we are here?" asked Maxine.
"No, and I have been sworn to secrecy," said the driver.
The driver sorted the bags into the car and whisked them off quickly; it was almost like a big rush.
"Where are you taking us, to meet Lorraine?" asked Maxine.

"Lorraine and Steve's place to drop your bags off, then I will take you somewhere else immediately afterwards," said the driver.

"Where else?"

"Sorry, I've been told I can't say."

Maxine and Demetrio looked at each other; they both sensed that something was going on.

The House

They arrived at the house and were greeted by Susan. They gestured for the driver to put the bags in the corner, then asked what was going on and where Lorraine and Steve were.

"Lorraine wasn't feeling well, so the doctor has taken her to the hospital. They left a few hours ago. She's in a private room, and Lorraine's driver is going to take you there now." Said Susan.

"Oh my, oh no, is the baby, okay?" asked Maxine, now extremely worried.

"Yes, from what I know. Go to the hospital!"

"Come, Maxine, let's get there," said Demetrio.

Chapter-Fifty-Five
McMatters

McMatters was pacing anxiously outside the hospital room, where Lorraine lay, now connected to a myriad of monitors, that beeped and whirred ominously. The sterile smell of antiseptic filled the air around him, almost suffocating in its intensity. His heart raced as he felt an overwhelming sense of helplessness wash over him.

He didn't know what to do first, or who to contact; every thought seemed to collide into another, creating a chaotic whirlwind in his mind. For the first time in his life, he felt utterly lost and disoriented, grappling with an insidious worry, that gnawed at him relentlessly. The feeling of being unable to control the situation was profoundly unsettling; it loomed over him like a dark cloud threatening rain at any moment.

"Steve! Steve!" Called Jarvis, as he arrived with Katrina. He took hold of McMatters and guided him out of the area, then out of the building. Katrina went in to see Lorraine.

"Steve, what's the score? Tell me everything and I will go digging," said Jarvis.

"Lorraine hadn't been feeling great, getting bad pains when eating. After they took her blood pressure, they found it was high…. like, too high. Proteins in water…. I've no idea what that means, so they brought her in," said McMatters.

"OK, when does Maxine arrive?"

"They are on their way and should be here soon."

"Let's go back in until they arrive."

McMatters had finally ceased his incessant pacing, but the tension that radiated from him was palpable. He remained visibly on edge, a coiled spring ready to unleash at any moment. Jarvis felt a creeping sense of unease wash over him; he couldn't shake the fear of what McMatters might do if things took a turn for the worse.

At that moment, it felt as though McMatters was a ticking time bomb, teetering on the brink of an explosive reaction. The air around them was thick with anxiety, and each passing minute only intensified Jarvis's worries. After what felt like an eternity of waiting, thirty long minutes later, Maxine and Demetrio arrived....it was good to have Lorraine's mum there, in this tumultuous situation. With their presence providing a semblance of reassurance amidst the chaos, McMatters and Jarvis swiftly set off to seek answers from the doctors, who held crucial information about Lorraine's condition.

They were desperate to understand the underlying concerns regarding the high blood pressure. Why was it such a significant issue? What could be lurking in the shadows that warranted such alarm? Moreover, there was also an unsettling question about why protein, detected in her water would raise red flags among medical professionals. Was it simply an indicator of something else? Every second felt precious, as they moved through sterile corridors filled with harsh fluorescent lights and distant echoes of hurried footsteps.... each one serving as a reminder of their pressing need for clarity in this unnerving situation.

Lorraine

"Mum! I'm so glad you're back home, but when did you arrive?" Lorraine asked, in surprise.
"We have only just arrived and came straight from the airport," said Maxine.
"Why didn't you tell me?"
"We were going to surprise you, but I think you surprised us."
"It looks like I have to stay in Hospital now until I have had the baby."

"You need the rest, Lorraine. Have they come to see you yet?"
"No, I've been told nothing. It's driving me crazy."
"Steve will find out, I'm sure."
"I'm going to go get you a few bits. If you're staying in, you'll need them."
"I will stay here with Lorraine," said Katrina.

The Doctor

"Doc, I need information," said McMatters.
"Hello, Mr McMatters. Lorraine's proteins are under observation. The imbalance can be caused by the pregnancy itself, so it is quite common. She would have had symptoms like fatigue, swelling of hands and feet, and abdominal pains," said the doctor.
"What about the blood pressure?" asked McMatters.
"The blood pressure is being monitored. This is due to hypertension after the 20-week mark. It can happen, and we are monitoring closely, because Lorraine might have the markers for pre-eclampsia, which comes with risks to both mother and baby. I won't sugar-coat it, Mr McMatters; it is quite possible this is the cause."
"Worst case scenario, please, doc? I need to be prepared."
"In the worst case, complications could happen when Lorraine is in labour. The baby could go into distress, Lorraine could bleed very badly, and we will be prepared for that, as too much blood loss could be fatal."
"Thank you, doc, for being honest."
"At this stage, the more rest and fluids, the better. She will be staying in, and we may have to induce labour and bring it forward."
"Is that safe?" asked Jarvis.
"It's safer in some cases. My current focus is on the pains she's describing. We are doing scans shortly to check what is happening when Lorraine eats, because it has been known for

the placenta to stop feeding the baby. If that's the case, labour will be induced immediately."

"Thank you, doc," said McMatters.

"Ok, Steve, first gather yourself. You can't go back in there looking worried and scared," said Jarvis.

"What on earth am I going to say to Lorraine?"

"Nothing, that's the doctor's job."

"I know, but…."

"No, it will increase her blood pressure and make it more dangerous. We all need to play it down for now and be positive. I know it will be hard."

"Thanks, Jarvis."

The Hospital Room

The hospital had a strict policy, that prevented everyone from visiting at the same time. This meant that they had to take turns, popping in to see Lorraine. It was a bit of a hassle really, but that's how it went. However, there was one person who simply wouldn't budge: McMatters. He was determined to stay by Lorraine's side no matter what. Every day, Jarvis would swing by with fresh clothes for him, and the hospital staff didn't mind too much. After all, he was shelling out a small fortune for that private room and all those endless tests, they kept running on Lorraine. Each time Lorraine managed to drift off into some much-needed sleep, it seemed like the nurses were right there, ready to wake her up again for yet another round of tests. It felt like they had no regard for her rest at all! McMatters grew increasingly worried about how little sleep she was getting, because of all the disturbances …. it just didn't seem fair. And then there were those late-night visits! At 3 am one morning, they came in and woke up McMatters!

"Excuse me," the nurse whispered, "the doctor needs to speak with you outside."

McMatters left the room, and upon seeing the doctor's face, he knew something was wrong.

"Lorraine is going up to the delivery suite now. We need to induce labour immediately; the placenta isn't feeding the baby. If we can't induce labour, she'll need a C-section. We're hoping labour is induced, though."

"Can I be there?" asked McMatters.

"In the labour room, yes. If it's a C-section, no, as that is classed as surgery," said the doctor.

McMatters phoned Jarvis. "Jarvis, they are taking her up. Can you make the calls, please?"

"No problem, see you soon."

Chapter Fifty-Six
Labour Induction

In the delivery suite, Steve was right there by Lorraine's side, holding her hand tightly. It was one of those moments that felt both surreal and incredibly real all at once. They had just kicked off the induction process, and he could see her face contort as she winced at the sharp pangs of pain that accompanied the procedure. Each time it happened, his heart ached for her; he wished he could take away even a fraction of her discomfort.

The room was filled with a mix of quiet determination and nervous anticipation, as they both knew they were on the brink of welcoming their little one into the world. The beeping machines and hushed voices only added to the weight of the moment, but all Steve could focus on was Lorraine's grip on his hand…. a silent testament to their shared journey through this beautiful chaos.

"How long does it take?" Asked McMatters
"From minutes to days; it depends. Lorraine will be having two sweeps in a short time frame to speed up the process," said the nurse.
"Soon the baby will be here, Lorraine," said McMatters.
"OK Lorraine, when labour starts, we'll give you pain relief. I have questions about which you'd prefer, depending on how quickly you start. Pethidine is the most common; it's an injection safe for the baby and stops the pain. Sometimes a few of these are needed as it has a short duration. Is that, OK?"
"Yes," said Lorraine.
"The other option is an epidural. It's an injection given in the lower spine area; it completely numbs you, but we need to administer it at the start of slow labour because it takes time to take effect. What are your thoughts?"
"If you think it's needed, then yes."

"I think it may be needed because we noticed a bend in your cervix and tailbone. Has it been damaged before?"

"Yes, when I was younger, I fell on a piece of metal on the bone."

"That must have been painful. Did you go to hospital?"

"No, I didn't see a doctor either."

"OK, so yes, I recommend the epidural, and we'll work the Pethidine around it. OK, let's check how far you are."

"3 cm currently," said the nurse.

"How many centimetres does she need to be?" asked McMatters.

"Ten for labour, but the epidural will be done at 5 cm. It can be done at any time, but as we're inducing, we'll do it in stages."

The nurse left the room, and it was just the two of them.

"Do you need anything, Lorraine?" asked McMatters.

"Can my mum be here too?" asked Lorraine.

"I will ask."

When McMatters stepped outside the room, he was greeted by the sight of Jarvis and Katrina, making their way towards him. It felt like a breath of fresh air to see some familiar faces.... well, they were more like family than just friends, really. Their presence instantly lightened his mood. Just behind them, however, was Maxine, who was quite the opposite; she was practically sprinting and looking all flustered, as she tried to keep up with the others. Her frantic energy suggested that something had her in a tizzy. Meanwhile, Demetrio ambled along at a relaxed pace, exuding an air of calmness, as if he knew all too well, that rushing about would do nothing to alleviate their concerns, or hurry things along. It seemed like he had adopted a philosophy, that sometimes it's best to take things in your stride, rather than let panic dictate one's speed.

McMatters was just happy to see everyone. They all nipped in one by one to see Lorraine; the nurse said they could, but they would need to be quick. She also mentioned that Maxine could be there, but both had the task of keeping Lorraine calm, with no anxiety, to maintain her blood pressure and minimise risks. Everyone managed to see Lorraine before the next induction.

The nurse strolled in to carry out her routine checks, casually announcing,

"5cm, we can do the epidural now."

Just then, a man entered the room holding a needle that looked almost comically oversized, so large, that it sent Maxine into a bit of a tailspin. One moment she was sitting there, and the next, she just dropped like a sack of potatoes.... completely out cold! The nurse sprang into action without missing a beat. She scooped Maxine up and gently plopped her onto a nearby chair, as if she were handling an oversized doll. It took what felt like an eternity for Maxine to regain her senses and piece together what had just unfolded around her. A mixture of surprise and embarrassment washed over her, as reality slowly came back into focus.

"It seems you can't look at needles, so I'll need you to step out while we do this," said the nurse.

Maxine reluctantly slipped out of the room, leaving Lorraine alone with the man handling the epidural. He handed her a special letter, that she needed to sign, and Lorraine felt a flutter of anxiety as she took it from him. With her spine bent awkwardly, he explained, that he couldn't inject in the safest spot, as he typically would. Instead, they had to go higher up her back, which brought with it an unsettling risk of paralysis.... a thought that sent a shiver down her spine. Despite the weight of what she was agreeing to, Lorraine took a deep breath, steeling herself for whatever came next. She grabbed the pen and quickly signed the document, her heart racing as she did so.

The man gave her the injection, and the nurse gently helped Lorraine back onto the bed with care. An hour later, Lorraine was feeling completely numb; even if she had wanted to, she couldn't lift her leg at all. It was an odd sensation, almost as if her body had become a heavy weight, that she couldn't control. In addition to that, Lorraine felt incredibly woozy and found it difficult to focus on anything around her. She kept glancing at the clock, trying to tell the time....an innocent task, that suddenly seemed like a monumental challenge....as she continuously lost track of the numbers swirling in her mind. How long had she been stuck in this delivery suite? The thought nagged at her like an itch just out of reach. If only she could muster up the strength to ask someone about it! But every time she opened her mouth to speak, the words tumbled out in a jumbled mess, that made no sense whatsoever. Frustration washed over her as she struggled to remember what exactly it was that she wanted to say in the first place; everything felt foggy and distant as if wrapped in a thick mist that wouldn't lift.

"8cm, we are on the road to labour, Mr McMatters."
"Call me Steve, please."
"Steve, you will soon be a daddy." Steve dashed to the door to announce Lorraine was in labour, and everyone cheered. Maxine went back inside with him.

Chapter Fifty-Seven
Labour

The contractions were becoming more frequent and stronger, each wave surging through Lorraine with increasing intensity. She had reached a significant milestone, measuring at 9 cm, which marked her progress in this profound journey, of bringing new life into the world. The atmosphere in the room was charged with a mix of anticipation and urgency, as many more doctors and nurses gathered around, each one meticulously preparing for the crucial moments that lay ahead. Their hushed voices flowed in and out like a gentle tide, punctuated by the reassuring beeps of the monitors, that tracked Lorraine's vital signs.

"Excuse me," the nurse said to Maxine, "since you fainted with the needle, I need to make sure you are okay with blood. Could you come over here, and we will check?"

The nurse pricked her finger and squeezed until blood came through, causing Maxine to faint.
"She can't stay in here," the doctor said, bringing her around and taking her to the waiting room.

At a mere 10 centimetres, the intensity of the contractions escalated dramatically, becoming increasingly powerful with each passing wave. Each time a contraction surged through Lorraine, McMatters found himself in a painful struggle, as he did his utmost to support and comfort her during this challenging moment. Unfortunately, this meant that his hand was often crushed in the grip of sheer intensity. The physical pressure he experienced, was not just a minor discomfort, but rather a testament to the overwhelming force of labour, underscoring the profound connection and shared experience of pain and strength between him and his Lorraine.

"OK Lorraine, it's getting closer to the time where I will tell you to push. I will also tell you to rest as well. Are you still with me Lorraine?"

"Yes!" Lorraine screamed as another contraction came.

It was two hours before the momentous occasion, when the baby would finally be welcomed into the world, a time filled with both anticipation and hope. The atmosphere was thick with emotion, as every heartbeat seemed to resonate with the promise of new life. Each passing minute felt like an eternity, yet there was an undeniable sense of calm amidst the flurry of activity…. a quiet understanding that soon, they would all witness a miracle unfold before their eyes.

"You've got this, Lorraine. I love you," said McMatters.

Lorraine was exhausted; all she could do was nod to show she felt the same way.

"OK, Lorraine, push now! Go!" shouted the nurse.

Lorraine poured her heart and soul into every moment of her labour, determined to bring her precious baby into the world. As she lay there, filled with a mixture of anticipation and anxiety, she watched as the medical team gently took her new-born to the side. A wave of confusion washed over her; in that fleeting moment, she couldn't quite understand what they were doing with her tiny bundle of joy. The atmosphere was charged with emotion, each second feeling like an eternity. Then, breaking through the tension, like a ray of sunshine piercing through clouds, came the unmistakable cries…sharp and high-pitched…. filling the room with life and signalling, that her little one had arrived safely. Those cries were not just sounds; they were a symphony of relief and overwhelming love, that resonated deeply within Lorraine's heart.

"Lorraine, you have a lovely baby boy!"

"Code Red," the nurse exclaimed as she hit the button.

But Lorraine couldn't focus; she was struggling deeply, caught in a web of confusion and distress. Something was undeniably wrong, an unsettling feeling gnawing at her insides like an unwelcome visitor. The distant wail of sirens pierced through the air, their urgent cries echoing like a haunting reminder of chaos unfolding nearby. As she glanced towards the window, the sight of red flashing lights danced erratically against the darkness, casting eerie shadows, that seemed to flicker with her waning strength. With each passing moment, she found herself fighting to keep her eyelids from succumbing to heaviness; it felt as though a weighted blanket was pressing down on her weary body, urging her to surrender to fatigue. Desperation clawed at her heart, as she grappled with the overwhelming sensation, that something far beyond her control was taking place around her.

"Lorraine! ... Lorraine!" McMatters shouted.
The nurse began to strike Lorraine's face... a distressing sight that made McMatters' heart sink with concern. It was a scene, that no one should have to witness, particularly in a place meant for healing. Despite the room being filled with doctors and nurses, all trained professionals who had committed their lives to caring for others, the nurse persisted in her alarming actions, seemingly oblivious to the turmoil unfolding around them. Each slap echoed not just in the air, but deeply within McMatters' mind, amplifying an overwhelming sense of urgency and helplessness. As anxiety washed over him, he felt an instinctive urge to intervene; after all, this was a moment where compassion and care were needed most. Was this truly happening? In that moment of chaos, it became painfully clear that something had gone terribly wrong.

"Stay with us, Lorraine!" shouted the nurse.
"What's happening?" McMatters was shouting now.
"We can't stop the bleeding; it's too much, too fast. Hang more blood!"

Lorraine desperately attempted to open her eyes, to shake off the enveloping darkness, that threatened to consume her, but despite her best efforts, she found herself unable to do so. The world around her began to fade into shadows, as she felt the warmth of life slip away, a direct consequence of the significant loss of blood, that coursed through her veins. In that harrowing moment, the once vivid scenes of her surroundings transformed into an inky void. The weight of exhaustion and pain pressed heavily upon her, and as if in response to an unrelenting fatigue, she succumbed to unconsciousness. Her heart raced in a futile attempt to hold on, but ultimately it was not enough; with each heartbeat growing weaker, she felt herself surrendering completely to the overwhelming darkness.

"Do something," said McMatters.
"Mr McMatters, you need to let us work. Outside, please?"

They took McMatters outside and shut the door.
McMatters couldn't move or speak. His life was uplifted one minute by his new baby boy …. but shattered with Lorraine now fighting for her life.

Chapter Fifty-Eight
The waiting room

Jarvis witnessed the unsettling scene unfold before him, as he watched them practically hurl McMatters out of the waiting delivery suite, with an alarming abruptness. It was a sight that sent a chill down his spine. McMatters stood there, utterly still, his body seemingly frozen in place, neither moving nor uttering a single word. The silence surrounding him was deafening, filled with an unspoken tension, that hung heavily in the air.

Jarvis felt a knot form in his stomach, as an instinctive sense of dread washed over him.... he knew something was terribly wrong. The look on McMatters' face was one of shock and confusion, illuminated by the harsh fluorescent lights, and it left Jarvis grappling with worry about what had just transpired within those sterile walls. The atmosphere had shifted dramatically, and fear clawed at his thoughts, as he pondered the implications of this distressing turn of events.

"Steve! What's wrong? What's happening?" asked Jarvis, who was now standing next to his best friend, turning McMatters to face him.

"Oh no, what's wrong? The baby? Lorraine?" Maxine went into panic mode, pacing and crying, unsure of what to do with herself.

McMatters was like a statue, as Jarvis guided him to the seats and sat him down.

"Steve, tell me what has just happened," asked Jarvis.

"I... I have a baby boy! But Lorraine......" the tears flowed; Jarvis had never seen McMatters cry before.

"Oh no, not Lorraine," cried Maxine. "What is happening with Lorraine, Steve?"

"She's losing too much blood; they can't stop the bleeding. She passed out, and the nurse was slapping her face to keep her awake, but it didn't work." The tears kept falling, his body now shuddering.

Fifty minutes later, a nurse and doctor came out, and everyone practically jumped up.

"Lorraine has suffered extreme blood loss. She has had a total of 6 pints of blood transfused, with 3 pints just to keep her with us. Lorraine is now very ill; she has stopped bleeding, but is struggling to wake up. This is quite normal; it's the body's way of protecting her so she can recover. We don't know how long it will take for Lorraine to wake up," added the doctor.

"You have a healthy baby boy weighing 5lb 6oz. As he is premature, he will spend 4 weeks in the premature baby unit minimum. We will take you there to see him soon," said the nurse.

"Mr McMatters, if you would like to come with me, I will take you to see Lorraine. When you come out, a nurse will come and take another family member in," said the doctor.

Steve followed the doctor, his tears now dry, but his eyes still red and sore from the grief that had overwhelmed him. As he stepped into the room, an unsettling wave of anxiety washed over him, causing his heart to flutter painfully in his chest. The moment he laid eyes on Lorraine, his heart melted in a way, that was both beautiful and heart-breaking. She looked so very pale, her skin seemingly drained of all colour, as she lay there connected to a series of monitors, that beeped rhythmically around her. Each beep felt like a reminder of the fragility of life, echoing in the silence that surrounded him. The sterile scent of antiseptic filled the air, mingling with an overwhelming sense of dread, as Steve took in every detail… the way her chest rose and fell with laboured breaths and how the faint beeping seemed to punctuate the weighty silence between them.

"What are all these monitors?"
"Lorraine currently has a drip, fluids, blood transfusion, blood pressure monitor, and heart rate monitor. It's crucial we

do all this as quickly as possible, as it will speed up her recovery," said the doctor.

"Is she OK? Will she be, OK?" asked McMatters.

"She should make a full recovery; we just don't know when. The nurse will now take you, with the baby, down to the premature unit," said the doctor.

As McMatters anxiously trailed behind the nurse, who carefully wheeled his baby, nestled in an incubator, towards the premature unit, a heavy sense of dread sat in his stomach. The beeping machines and sterile scent of antiseptic filled the air, amplifying his worries for his little one's wellbeing. Meanwhile, a different nurse led Maxine away to see Lorraine, leaving a palpable tension hanging in the air. Jarvis hurried after McMatters; concern etched on his face as he sensed the gravity of the situation. Katrina remained with Demetrio, her heart racing as they both waited to see Lorraine; each tick of the clock felt like an eternity, heightening their anxiety as they clung on to hope, amidst this uncertainty.

Maxine

Maxine was engulfed in a whirlwind of fear, worry, and overwhelming anxiety, regarding her daughter's current state. The weight of her concerns pressed heavily upon her chest, as she fervently wished for Lorraine to awaken and behold the innocent face of her new baby boy. It wasn't just about the immediate concern; it was about the emotional connection, that seemed to hang by a thread, one that had long been frayed throughout Lorraine's troubled childhood. Maxine felt a profound ache in her heart, knowing that she had failed to compensate for those lost years, when she should have been a source of love and support.

Now, standing at the precipice of what could be a momentous turning point in their relationship, Maxine was resolute…. this was the time for redemption. She would do absolutely anything within her power to help coax her daughter back from the brink of unconsciousness. The thought of seeing Lorraine's smile again, was not merely a desire, but an urgent necessity; it represented hope and healing, not just for Lorraine, but also for Maxine herself. With every passing moment, she recalled memories of laughter they had shared during better days, moments when they were closer, before life complicated their bond with shadows of regret and misunderstanding.

Maxine gently pressed her lips against her daughter's forehead, a tender gesture that spoke volumes about her love and concern. As she held Lorraine's small hand in her own, the weight of emotion bore down upon her, causing tears to spill silently down her cheeks, like raindrops tracing the contours of a windowpane. Each tear was a testament to the anguish, that clenched tightly around her heart, an overwhelming blend of fear and hope.

"Come on, Lorraine. Please wake up," Maxine whispered softly, her voice barely above a breath. The desperation in her tone, resonated with the stillness of the room, where time seemed suspended, as if holding its breath alongside Maxine. The world outside carried on with its usual noise and chaos, yet in this intimate moment between mother and daughter, everything else faded into insignificance.

The Baby

Jarvis stood quietly beside McMatters, both men enveloped in a heavy atmosphere of uncertainty, as they gazed at the fragile figure of McMatters' new baby boy. The tiny infant lay peacefully in his incubator, a feeding tube delicately attached to him, a reminder of the precariousness of life and the medical challenges that still lay ahead. Jarvis felt an unsettling knot form in his stomach, an ache born from ignorance. He had no idea how long this feeding tube would be necessary, or what other hurdles the little one might face on his journey to health.

As he glanced over at McMatters, Jarvis was struck by the deep concern etched across his friend's face. McMatters seemed lost in thought, vacantly staring into space, with eyes that held neither hope nor despair, but rather an unsettling void. It was clear that Lorraine's condition weighed heavily on him; she lay fighting her own battle nearby, and with each passing moment, Jarvis felt an increasing sense of helplessness for both father and son. Jarvis couldn't shake off the worry, that was gnawing at him.

How would McMatters navigate this tumultuous path if Lorraine didn't pull through? The thought loomed large in Jarvis's mind, like a dark cloud casting a shadow over their lives. Would McMatters possess the strength to cope with raising their new-born son alone? He imagined the overwhelming responsibilities, that would soon rest solely on McMatters' shoulders.... cradling a fragile life while grappling with immense grief and fear. The reality was daunting; nurturing a new-born required not only physical care, but also emotional resilience.... a quality that can be hard to summon in times of crisis. As his heart swelled with empathy for his friend, Jarvis wished desperately for answers and solutions that could ease this burden. In that moment, he knew they needed each other more than ever....and perhaps together they could find some semblance of strength amidst such uncertainty.

"Tomorrow, you can hold him, Mr McMatters," said the nurse.
"Really? But he's so small. Won't I hurt him?" asked McMatters.
"No, you'll be fine. He will be fine. Have you held a new born baby before?" asked the nurse.
"No."

"We will show you how to hold, change, and feed him. Do you have a name yet?"
"A name? Ummm, I can't pick. I need Lorraine."

The nurse smiled warmly, her eyes reflecting genuine kindness, before turning and walking away, leaving McMatters to his own thoughts in the quiet corridor. In that fleeting moment of solitude, he found himself enveloped by a swirling mix of emotions.... relief mingled with anxiety....as he contemplated the numerous challenges that lay ahead. The gentle hum of fluorescent lights above seemed to create a soothing backdrop for his reflections, while the faint scent of antiseptic lingered in the air, a reminder of his current surroundings. As he leaned against the cool wall, memories flooded back; moments when uncertainty had felt overwhelming and yet somehow manageable. He recalled times when small victories had brought him joy amidst turmoil.
Now, however, standing alone in that seemingly endless corridor, filled with echoes of distant footsteps and muffled voices, those memories felt both comforting and daunting. What did tomorrow hold? The uncertainty loomed like a shadow over him....

"Let's go to see Lorraine; Steve and Maxine can come to see the baby," urged Jarvis.

As they approached the lift, ready to return to the delivery suite, a palpable sense of anticipation filled the air around Maxine, Demetrio, and Katrina. The lift doors stood before them, like an entrance to a new world, where joy and love awaited just beyond its steel confines. Their hearts raced with emotion. This moment would mark a significant milestone in their lives and the beginning of countless cherished memories together, as they prepared to embrace this tiny miracle.

"Any change?" asked McMatters.

"No, not yet," said Maxine. "How's my grandchild?"
"He's great; they said I can hold him tomorrow." McMatters smiled at this.
"Oh wow, that's great news. Think positive, Steve. Lorraine is strong; she will be okay," said Maxine.

Chapter Fifty-Nine
Home

It had been an astonishing three weeks since Lorraine had brought a new life into the world, and now McMatters stood at a crossroads, tasked with the weighty responsibility of choosing his son's name. The air around him was thick with emotion; Lorraine still lay peacefully in her hospital bed, seemingly untouched by time, as she remained ensconced in what the doctors described as a mild coma. Yet, amidst this uncertainty, they offered glimmers of hope...signs that she might soon awaken from this deep slumber. They reassured him and urged him to think of it, not as a perilous situation, but rather as an extended rest, akin to being lost in a dream. As he prepared for this monumental decision beneath the flickering fluorescent lights of the registry office, McMatters felt both exhilarated and daunted by his role as a father.

The weight of expectation rested heavily on his shoulders; he knew that a name is more than just letters strung together.... it's an identity, a legacy waiting to unfold.
After much reflection and soul-searching through countless possibilities, swirling in his mind like autumn leaves caught in the wind, he finally arrived at a name that resonated deeply within him: Lucifer James McMatters. The choice was strikingly bold and filled with significance.... a testament to both light and dark, intertwined within human experience. With each syllable echoing through his thoughts, he felt an exhilarating rush; naming his son was not merely about tradition or conformity, but rather about embracing individuality and courage. And so, with trembling hands, yet an unwavering resolve, McMatters stepped forward into this new chapter of his life.... first though it was time to collect his son from the hospital.
In the astonishing span of just three weeks, he had undergone a remarkable transformation, evolving from a life defined by brutality.... breaking bones and slitting throats....to

embracing the tender and nurturing responsibilities of fatherhood. Now, he found himself immersed in an entirely different realm: learning the delicate art of crafting a bottle, expertly changing nappies, and providing the loving care, that his precious son so desperately needed. The anticipation was palpable; as soon as he collected his little one today, he would not only register his son's name, but would also take immense pride in showcasing this beautiful new chapter of his life to the world. The very thought filled him with exhilaration and joy.... he could barely contain his eagerness!

Jarvis was set to accompany him today, a twist of fate that felt almost magical during their challenging circumstances. Meanwhile, Katrina and Maxine were planning to visit Lorraine, eager to offer their support and companionship. It was truly heart-warming, to witness how everyone was selflessly taking turns to be with Lorraine during this trying time; each visit served as a beacon of hope amidst the uncertainty. They all shared a collective wish.... a deep-seated longing...that Lorraine would wake up and re-join them, bringing back her vibrant spirit and the laughter, that had always illuminated their lives. The thought of seeing her eyes flicker open once again, filled them with an indescribable sense of anticipation and hope, akin to waiting for the first light of dawn after a long night.

Chapter Sixty
Living

Little baby Lucifer James McMatters had already blossomed into a delightful 24 days old child. His proud parent, McMatters, cherished every single moment spent with his precious little one; wherever he went, Lucifer was sure to be right there by his side, like a loyal companion in this beautiful journey of parenthood. With each passing day, McMatters had become quite the expert in the art of changing nappies…. a sometimes messy yet always rewarding task….and had even mastered the acrobatics involved in dressing a tiny baby, without causing too much fuss. He couldn't help but chuckle at Paulie's unique and entertaining approach to preparing baby bottles; it was nothing short of an amusing spectacle. With an almost cocktail-like flair, Paulie would expertly shake and swirl the bottle before expertly rolling it across the counter, as if putting on a show just for little Lucifer's amusement. Today was especially significant, as they were on their way to see Lorraine, having received a call from the hospital, that filled them both with hope and anticipation. Maybe at last there was some sign of improvement in Lorraine's current state of coma. The prospect of seeing her again, filled their hearts with warmth and optimism amidst a backdrop of uncertainty.

Hospital

McMatters, cradling little Lucifer snugly in his car seat, strode through the hospital doors with a heart full of hope and joy. As he made his way into the ward where Lorraine was being cared for, he was met by an enthusiastic chorus of nurses who gathered around him. Their eyes sparkled with delight as they cooed over the tiny bundle of joy, that was Lucifer, their excitement palpable in the air. Each smile and gentle remark added to McMatter's buoyant spirits, as he continued towards the private room. When he finally reached

Lorraine's room, he pushed open the door with a mix of anticipation and trepidation…. but then time seemed to stand still.

There she was…. awake! The sight of Lorraine's eyes fluttering open filled him with an overwhelming sense of elation. After twenty-four long days, since she had brought their precious son into the world and fallen into a coma, it felt like a miracle to see her conscious again! The weight that had been pressing down on his heart began to lift as pure joy surged within him; McMatters could hardly believe his eyes. He was utterly over the moon!

"Lorraine, oh my God," McMatters was shocked. "I'm so glad you're awake. We missed you so much." He leaned in and kissed Lorraine on the head.
"Baby, is the baby, OK?"
"Lucifer is perfect, Lorraine, just like you."
McMatters went out to the nurses' station, collects Lucifer, and brings him into the room. "And here is Lucifer," said McMatters as he takes him out of the car seat. "Lucifer, meet your mummy."
McMatters places Lucifer in her arms, tears rolling down her face. "How?" Lorraine was still woozy. "You named him?"
"Yes, I couldn't keep calling him 'baby' or 'little guy.'"
"What's his full name?"
"Lucifer James McMatters."
"I love it, Steve."
"When you had him, there were complications. You lost a lot of blood, and they had to fight to keep you with us. When you passed out, I was thrown out of the room, and not long after, you were in a coma."
"How long have I been here?"
"You have been sleeping for 24 days. We have all been taking turns coming every day, just waiting for you to wake up."
"You looked after him?"
"Yes, I did. I learnt a lot about babies. I am a modern man."

Lorraine laughed, though she was still quite weak, but she was awake, and that's all that mattered. Lorraine whispered,

"So, Mr Criminal Mastermind also changes nappies?"
"I do indeed. I have been teaching him various skills, thanks to Paulie, and he can do acrobatics while getting dressed, and laughs when we make bottle cocktails."
Lorraine really laughed at this. She couldn't wait to go home.
"When can I go home?"
"I need to talk with the doctor." He picked up Lucifer and walked to the door. "Can the doctor come by, please? She's awake, and we have a few questions."
"Lorraine, I do love you so much. You're awake and alive, and that's all that matters.... well, that and getting you home."
"I love you too. I am so tired right now; I might just have a sleep."
"Rest, honey. I'm not going anywhere."

McMatters picks up the phone, bubbling with joy and a sense of exhilaration, that is simply infectious. With a heart full of enthusiasm, he can barely contain himself, as he prepares to share the wonderful news. It's as if he wants to shout it from the rooftops, letting everyone know that Lorraine has finally awakened! The sheer delight in McMatter's voice radiates through each word, painting a vivid picture of his excitement and eagerness, to spread this uplifting message far and wide. It's not just an announcement; it's a celebration of life and hope, a moment that deserves to be shared with all those who know and care about Lorraine!

The End

Awakening

After awakening from her coma, Lorraine finds herself engulfed in a whirlwind of emotions, grappling with the challenges of adjusting to life after the birth of her son, Lucifer. This internal conflict weighs heavily on her heart and mind, leading her to contemplate a drastic choice, that could alter the course of both their lives forever. In stark contrast to Lorraine's turmoil, McMatters revels in the joys of fatherhood and arrives at a life-changing decision, that could redefine his future. As fate would have it, wedding bells begin to toll for them amidst this emotional backdrop. Meanwhile, Demetrio and Maxine are also taking significant steps forward in their relationship, as romance blossoms around them. With all these developments unfolding against a backdrop filled with excitement and anticipation, one must ponder: what lies ahead for Dreams Night Club? What's next in Jarvis and Katrina's relationship?

Coming soon

Printed in Great Britain
by Amazon